Midnight Untamed

Also from Lara Adrian

Midnight Breed Series

A Touch of Midnight (prequel novella FREE eBook)
Kiss of Midnight
Kiss of Crimson
Midnight Awakening
Midnight Rising
Veil of Midnight
Ashes of Midnight
Shades of Midnight
Taken by Midnight
Deeper Than Midnight
A Taste of Midnight (ebook novella)
Darker After Midnight
The Midnight Breed Series Companion
Edge of Dawn
Marked by Midnight (novella)
Crave the Night
Tempted by Midnight (novella)
Bound to Darkness
Stroke of Midnight
Defy the Dawn
Midnight Untamed
...and more to come!
Also:
The Midnight Breed Series Coloring Book

The 100 Series (billionaire contemporary romance)

For 100 Days
For 100 Nights (forthcoming)
For 100 Reasons (forthcoming)

Masters of Seduction Series
Merciless: House of Gravori
Priceless: House of Ebarron

Phoenix Code Series (with Tina Folsom)
Cut and Run (Books 1 & 2)
Hide and Seek (Books 3 & 4)

Historical Romances

Dragon Chalice Series
Heart of the Hunter (FREE eBook)
Heart of the Flame
Heart of the Dove
Dragon Chalice Boxed Set

Warrior Trilogy
White Lion's Lady (FREE eBook)
Black Lion's Bride
Lady of Valor
Warrior Trilogy Boxed Set

Standalone Titles
Lord of Vengeance

Midnight Untamed

A Midnight Breed Novella

By Lara Adrian

1001 Dark Nights

EVIL EYE
CONCEPTS

Midnight Untamed
A Midnight Breed Novella
By Lara Adrian

1001 Dark Nights
Copyright 2016 Lara Adrian
ISBN: 978-1-942299-59-2

Foreword: Copyright 2014 M. J. Rose
Published by Evil Eye Concepts, Incorporated

Acknowledgments from the Author

I am so excited to be part of the 1001 Dark Nights collection again with this new novella in my Midnight Breed vampire romance series. Thank you to Liz Berry, MJ Rose, Jillian Stein, and the rest of the creative, marketing, and editorial teams at Evil Eye Concepts for the incredible vision and enthusiasm you bring to each release in the collection. It's a pleasure to be working with all of you!

To my amazing readers, thank you for your continued support and for joining me on yet another adventure within the Midnight Breed story world. I hope you enjoy Savage and Bella's story, and all the rest still to come.

Happy reading!

Love, Lara

Sign up for the 1001 Dark Nights Newsletter
and be entered to win a Tiffany Key necklace.

There's a contest every month!

Go to www.1001DarkNights.com to subscribe.

As a bonus, all subscribers will receive a free
1001 Dark Nights story
The First Night
by Lexi Blake & M.J. Rose

One Thousand and One Dark Nights

Once upon a time, in the future…

*I was a student fascinated with stories and learning.
I studied philosophy, poetry, history, the occult, and
the art and science of love and magic. I had a vast
library at my father's home and collected thousands
of volumes of fantastic tales.*

*I learned all about ancient races and bygone
times. About myths and legends and dreams of all
people through the millennium. And the more I read
the stronger my imagination grew until I discovered
that I was able to travel into the stories… to actually
become part of them.*

*I wish I could say that I listened to my teacher
and respected my gift, as I ought to have. If I had, I
would not be telling you this tale now.
But I was foolhardy and confused, showing off
with bravery.*

*One afternoon, curious about the myth of the
Arabian Nights, I traveled back to ancient Persia to
see for myself if it was true that every day Shahryar
(Persian: شهریار, "king") married a new virgin, and then
sent yesterday's wife to be beheaded. It was written
and I had read, that by the time he met Scheherazade,
the vizier's daughter, he'd killed one thousand
women.*

Something went wrong with my efforts. I arrived in the midst of the story and somehow exchanged places with Scheherazade — a phenomena that had never occurred before and that still to this day, I cannot explain.

Now I am trapped in that ancient past. I have taken on Scheherazade's life and the only way I can protect myself and stay alive is to do what she did to protect herself and stay alive.

Every night the King calls for me and listens as I spin tales. And when the evening ends and dawn breaks, I stop at a point that leaves him breathless and yearning for more. And so the King spares my life for one more day, so that he might hear the rest of my dark tale.

As soon as I finish a story... I begin a new one... like the one that you, dear reader, have before you now.

Chapter 1

The palatial villa two hours outside Rome glittered like a jewel beneath the starlit night sky. Lights glowed from within the sprawling mansion and along the circular drive out front, where half a dozen sleek sports cars were parked on the cobbled stones.

From his vantage point on a tree-studded hill five hundred yards away, Ettore Selvaggio watched as a beautiful red Ferrari rolled up to the villa and took its place between a silver Bugatti Veyron and a blue Pagani Huayra. Add in the pair of Lamborghinis, the Maserati, and another Ferrari, and there was well over ten million dollars' of automotive luxury parked outside Vito Massioni's mansion. Plus a collection of vehicles worth twice that amount stowed inside the massive bays of the reputed drug-dealing Breed male's private garage.

If nothing else, Massioni and his criminal associates had impeccable taste in cars.

"Apparently, selling your soul to Opus Nostrum pays well," he muttered into the wireless mic that linked him to the Order's command center back in Rome. "You getting my visual on this place?"

"Visual acknowledged, Savage."

The deep gravel voice of his comrade, Trygg, was never easy to read, and tonight was no exception. Not that Savage actually expected the menacing warrior to appreciate the fleet of fine Italian machinery belonging to Massioni and his cohorts.

And not that it mattered, anyway.

In a few minutes, the cars, the mansion, and everyone in it would be nothing but ash and smoking rubble.

Damned shame about the cars.

"Status," Trygg prompted over the earpiece as Savage hunkered down to watch the coming fireworks.

"Packages have been delivered and the last party guest just arrived. We're good to go."

"You collected the receipt?"

"Right here in my pocket," he said, tapping the flash drive Trygg referenced.

Twenty minutes before Savage arrived at his observation position on the hill, he'd been inside Massioni's villa on a covert solo mission to download key computer data, then take out the target. According to intel newly obtained by the Order's headquarters in Washington, D.C., Vito Massioni was the European distributor of a dangerous narcotic that turned otherwise law-abiding Breed vampires into blood-obsessed, murderous Rogues.

This new drug with the street name Red Dragon was said to be even more powerful than its predecessor, Crimson, which had cost countless Breed and human lives when it hit the streets twenty years ago. Now, thanks to Massioni and his collusion with the terror group, Opus Nostrum, Rogue outbreaks were on the rise again in the States and across Europe, creating panic among an already anxious human public. As leader of the Order, Lucan Thorne had made it clear that he wanted the problem cut off at the source, and cut off swiftly.

Savage was more than happy to be tapped for the covert assignment. It had been a serendipitous bonus to learn that Massioni had called a private meeting with his lieutenants tonight. So, instead of a data grab and stealth assassination—one of many lethal specialties that had earned Savage his nickname in the Order—the scope of the job had expanded to mass elimination.

To that end, four explosive devices with enough firepower to level an entire city block were now planted around Massioni's villa. All Savage had to do was set them off by remote detonator and Opus would lose yet another key ally. The Order wasn't about to rest until the entire organization was dismantled, the cabal of members at its helm unmasked and destroyed.

Savage lifted his field glasses to his eyes and peered at the mansion. Although his vision as one of the Breed was superhuman, the lenses allowed him to zoom in on the illuminated window of the grand salon where Massioni and his men were gathered.

The seven Breed males evidently had plenty of cause for celebration. They greeted one another with a lot of laughter and back patting, a lot of ingratiating smiles and kowtowing for the dark-haired, hawk-nosed Vito Massioni from his underlings. No doubt the Red Dragon dealer and his cronies had been handsomely rewarded for their part in the spike of Rogue attacks the past few nights. Savage couldn't wait to send them all to their final reward tonight.

"Light it up at your ready," Trygg advised.

Savage smiled behind his binoculars. "With pleasure."

Glancing away from the meeting taking place inside the mansion, he reached to retrieve the remote detonator. Normally he didn't get invested in witnessing a target's demise, but it was hard not to take some satisfaction in crashing Massioni's little party tonight.

He brought the field glasses back up to his face—just in time to see that a woman had entered the room. The petite blonde wore a flashy red dress that clung to her slender body like liquid silk. The neckline plunged low in front, the slit in the skirt slicing high up her leg, baring a lot of creamy thigh with each gliding step she took toward Massioni.

What the fuck?

Savage hadn't realized there was a female in the mansion. Not that he felt much sympathy for anyone who associated with a thug like Massioni. And not that it should stop him from pushing the button on the detonator. But still...

His thumb froze, hovering over the trigger.

"Unidentified female on the premises," he murmured into his mic. "Stand by, base."

"Standing by," Trygg said. Then he made a low, appreciative noise that might as well have been a wolf-whistle, coming from the eternally inscrutable warrior.

Yeah, the female was hot. Savage barely contained his own primal growl at the sight of all those slender curves poured into a column of scarlet silk. He'd long avoided blondes—for personal reasons of his own—but everything male in him responded to the sight of this one like flame to gasoline.

He stared through the lenses, watching as every head in the room turned to look at her as she approached Massioni. As soon as she was close enough, the vampire's beefy arm snaked out to hook her around the waist, pulling her roughly against him as his buddies grinned and chuckled.

More than one of the Breed males gathered in the room wore an expression of unabashed lust as their boss crudely cupped the young woman's breast in front of them all.

A jab of disgust spiked through Savage's blood at Massioni's manhandling of the woman.

"There was no mention of a female in the intel," Trygg said.

"No, there wasn't." Savage's reply was clipped, irritation combined with this unwanted element of surprise. "The report out of D.C. specifically stated that Massioni is unmated, so who the fuck is she?"

"Collateral damage," Trygg replied evenly. "Pop the charges and get the hell out of there."

Savage nodded, knowing that was sound advice.

But his thumb didn't move on the detonator.

Something was starting to bother him about the woman the longer he stared at her. Something that gnawed at the perimeter of his memory.

"I need a closer look."

Without waiting for confirmation from his comrade, he set the detonator down in the soft grass, then tightened the focus on his binoculars. Not on Massioni or his men, but on her. The gorgeous blonde whose heart-shaped face and pixie features seemed strangely, distantly familiar somehow.

Which was impossible, considering this female was clearly Massioni's plaything.

The face that teased at the frayed edges of Savage's mind—and his heart—had no place here. Not with criminals and killers like the ones assembled inside the villa that was wired to blow on his command.

Holy shit.

It couldn't be her.

Trygg's voice sounded in his ear. "You got problems over there?"

Savage couldn't answer that. Not when his veins were filling with adrenaline and a sick feeling of apprehension was starting to take up space behind his sternum.

He brought the woman in closer, his eyes burning from the intensity of his unblinking stare. She was still caught within the cage of Massioni's thick arm, smiling indulgently as the Breed male showed her off like some kind of prize to his leering friends. Showing her off as if the bastard owned her.

Fuck. Don't let that be her.

"Status," Trygg demanded now. "What's going on?"

"I'm not sure. I think the woman is…" He drew in a breath, hoping like hell he was wrong. "Christ, I think I know her."

Trygg's curse scraped across the earpiece. "Bad fucking time for a reunion with one of your many conquests, man. And if the bitch belongs to our target, you don't know her now."

No, he didn't.

Not anymore.

Hell, not for a very long time.

As Savage watched, Massioni finally released the woman from his possessive hold. He said something to his colleagues, a remark that made them all chuckle. Then Massioni gestured at her dismissively. Her placid smile still in place, the beautiful blonde pivoted away from the men.

It wasn't until she turned around that Savage's suspicion was confirmed.

The proof was there on the back of her left shoulder—the scarlet mark of a Breedmate. Only the rarest of women bore the unique birthmark signifying they were something more than mortal.

The small teardrop-and-crescent-moon symbol rode this female's shoulder in the precise spot that Savage dreaded it would.

"Son of a bitch. I don't believe this."

It *was* her.

After all this time—nearly a decade.

Arabella Genova.

Savage snarled as Massioni playfully smacked her ass, sending her on her way. Unfazed, she glided out of the room as elegantly as she'd entered a few moments ago, Savage following her progress with the field glasses held in a grip so tight they should have shattered.

Trygg was right. He didn't know her now.

How the girl he once adored had ended up in the hands of a thug like Vito Massioni, he could only guess.

And it didn't matter.

Savage had a job to do.

That's what he told himself, even as he pulled the binoculars away from his face and hissed a sharp curse into the darkness.

The Bella he'd known as a girl all those years ago was just a memory. This Bella was in the wrong place at the wrong time, and on the dead wrong side of the law.

Collateral damage, just like Trygg said.

Savage knew what he had to do. The Order might never have the chance to get this close to Massioni and his lieutenants again. Everything was in place. The mission was moments away from success. All he had to do was hit the detonator.

He picked it up, staring at the trigger that would erase Massioni and his entire operation from the face of the Earth.

And, now, Bella too.

"Fuck."

Savage raked a hand over his tightly clamped jaw. His pulse was banging in his temples, his heart slamming against his ribs with each heavy beat.

"Status," Trygg said, a note of warning in the warrior's gravel voice. "I don't like what I'm hearing over there, Savage."

He didn't answer. Nothing he said now would put his comrade or anyone else at the command center in Rome at ease.

Savage set aside the binoculars. Then he carefully deactivated the detonator and slipped the remote into his back pocket.

"Stand by, base. I'm going back in."

Chapter 2

Arabella held her composure until she had reached her private quarters on the villa's second floor. Once inside, she leaned against the closed door and let her revulsion leak out of her on a shudder. At least she was getting better at the charade. There was a time when she might have had to bite back a scream.

Her skin crawled everywhere Vito had touched her. She could still feel his hard fingers on her body, on her breast. The sting of his offensive smack to her backside burned her dignity even more than it did her ass.

She hated being trotted out in front of his friends as his personal show pony, forced to dress and act as if she belonged to the coarse, criminal Breed male.

Though to be fair, in many ways Massioni did own her. Her life. Her freedom. Her unique Breedmate gift for premonition—the thing that first brought her to his attention three years ago. He owned all of that, no matter how much she despised him.

He might have owned her body, too, if she hadn't found a way to convince him that the price of taking that part of her would cost him the one thing he couldn't afford to lose.

The threat had kept her out of his reach so far, but there were times when she knew he'd been tempted to test her. She only hoped she wouldn't kill him if he tried. Because no matter how clever she wanted to think she was in dealing with him, Vito Massioni always had one final, terrible card to play.

And so long as he held that over her head, she had no choice but to serve him.

She could never escape him, not even in death.

He'd made certain of that.

Arabella knew better than to keep Massioni waiting. He'd sent her away to fetch her scrying bowl while he entertained his bootlicking cronies in the grand salon. They were gloating over a large payout from a shipment of Red Dragon to the States and the United Kingdom—a narcotic that destroyed the minds of their own kind, the Breed, creating blood-addicted monsters from just the smallest dose. They didn't care that their sudden windfall came at the expense of both Breed and human lives. She had learned a long time ago that Vito Massioni's greed knew no bounds.

Nor did his violence.

That her gift had helped him amass his growing fortune, and the power that came with it, made Arabella want to retch.

How often had she thought about giving him a false reading from her scrying bowl?

How many times had she dreaded that her visions would one day prove incorrect?

But she hadn't deceived him, not once.

And, thankfully, her visions had never been wrong.

Either of those failings would come at the cost of innocent lives. Not her own, but the people she cared about most in the world. The only family she had left now.

It was those precious lives she held close in her heart as she walked over to the cabinet across the room and retrieved the hammered gold bowl she would need for her reading downstairs. In reality, her gift would awaken when she peered into any standing pool of liquid, but Massioni insisted she use the ridiculous carnival fortune-teller's style bowl for dramatic effect whenever she performed a public reading.

Cradling the shallow bowl in her palms, she drew the empty vessel out of the cabinet. Her own face stared back at her in the reflection on the polished gold basin—but that wasn't all.

Behind her stood the ominous shape of someone else.

A man.

Tall, immense.

An intruder dressed entirely in black tactical gear.

Bella sucked in a startled breath.

Fear streaked through her, but before her shriek could rip up the back of her throat, a broad palm came up to cover her mouth.

Oh, God.

The bowl slipped out of her grasp, thudding onto the thick rug. Muscular arms caged her from behind, immobilizing her. She staggered on her high-heeled sandals, drawn helplessly against the unmistakable heat of a very strong, very male body.

Not Massioni's. This wasn't any of the other men gathered in the salon with him either, although there was no question that the male trapping her in his unbreakable hold was Breed.

"Don't scream, Bella."

He spoke against her ear, his growled command voiced in a deep baritone that brushed over her jangled senses like a caress.

He knew her name. How? Who the hell was he? Where had he come from?

She struggled and fought to break free, but he didn't let go. He was much too strong, and none of her squirming or resisting was getting her anywhere. All her grunts and cries for help were snuffed by the hand still sealed firmly across her lips.

Trapped, she could only stand there, her breath rushing out of her nose in panicked gusts while terror wrapped around her heart like a vise.

"Be calm. I'm not going to hurt you."

Did he think she was a fool? She didn't believe him for a second, not when she could feel the lethal power radiating off his big body. Whoever this man was, he was beyond dangerous, and she had no doubt that his only business in the villa was death.

She groaned, trying futilely to pull away from him in another burst of desperation. Her heart was speeding, banging against her rib cage as if on the verge of exploding. Yet despite her alarm, her instincts had begun to prickle with some kind of distant recognition.

She knew it was impossible, this strange feeling that this intruder was no stranger at all. Her blood was still racing and cold with terror, but beneath the fear was a growing sense of familiarity.

A name skated across her memory, one she had tried for years to bar from her thoughts and her heart.

No. It couldn't be him.

The beautiful, golden-haired Breed male she had known all those years ago had been a scholar, not a soldier. He would have no business in a place like this, among thugs like the ones gathered downstairs.

Then again, there was a time when she'd have said the same thing about herself.

"I'm going to remove my hand from your mouth now," he murmured.

As he spoke, his breath skimmed warmly against her cheek and along the side of her neck. She shivered from the sensation, astonished to realize how deeply he affected her, even after all this time.

Because, yes, she did know that low, velvet voice.

Just as she knew the scent that enveloped her as she stood immobilized in his arms. Heaven help her, but she had carried the scent of him, the sound of his voice, in a private corner of her heart since she was a teenage girl.

"Don't be afraid, Bella. I didn't come here to harm you. Nod your head if you understand."

She nodded, and his grip on her relaxed. His palm fell away from her lips, leaving a coldness in its wake. Arabella slowly turned around in his slack hold.

"Oh, my God." The words leaked out of her on a disbelieving sigh. "Ettore."

Even though she thought she was prepared to see him again now, her first glimpse of Ettore Selvaggio standing mere inches away from her was a complete shock to her system.

She brought her fingers to her lips, her fear replaced by an overwhelming feeling of incredulity...and confusion.

Although she knew his voice and scent, she barely recognized the hard, disapproving face that stared back at her.

A black knit skullcap covered the loose golden waves that would have framed his lean, angled cheeks and firm, square jaw. While she knew that when he smiled there were dimples on either side of his lush mouth, right now his sculpted lips were held in a grim, unforgiving line. His hazel eyes were intense, his brows lowering as he pinned her in a measuring stare that felt as dangerous and unyielding as his hold on her a moment ago.

"Jesus Christ," he whispered on a sharp exhalation. His expression hardened even more. "It really is you, Arabella. I had to be sure. I didn't want to believe it."

She frowned. He sounded as surprised to see her as she was to be looking at him.

It had been ten years since they last saw each other. Ten years since he crushed her heart and walked away, never to return. Now, here he stood, dressed like a nightmare in black combat gear and staring at her in accusation, as if she were the one to blame.

His gaze seared her, making her feel cold and exposed in the curve-hugging red silk dress Massioni insisted she wear tonight. She knew what she must look like, what Ettore must think.

As much as everything inside her urged her to explain, she had bigger things to worry about than his opinion of her now.

"What the hell do you think you're doing? How did you get in here?" She couldn't hide the shock in her voice, or her dread. If Massioni or any of his guards discovered Ettore inside the villa, they would kill him. And Bella didn't doubt for a second that she would be made to suffer too. "Are you insane? Get out of here now, Ettore. You have no idea how dangerous it is for you to be here."

He gave her a smile that chilled. "I'm not the one in danger. Your lover and his cronies are. I've rigged this place to blow sky-high as soon as I hit the detonator in my pocket."

Oh, God. She swallowed, stricken to hear him admit what she'd already guessed. He was here to kill Vito Massioni.

And she could not let that happen.

Because if Massioni died, he had promised that she and her remaining family would die too.

A muffled rumble of laughter carried from the salon downstairs. Massioni and his guests would be growing restless soon. She'd already been gone too long. She couldn't risk anyone coming to look for her.

No more than she could risk allowing Ettore the chance to carry out what he'd come here tonight to do.

"I'm sorry," she murmured, shaking her head as she took a step away from him. "I'm sorry… Ettore, I have no choice."

Before he could stop her—before he probably even guessed what she was about to do—Bella screamed at the top of her lungs.

Chapter 3

There was barely a second of silence between the sound of Bella's scream and the pandemonium that followed.

Male voices shouted from the salon below. Heavy boot falls began to thunder from all directions, while outside, perimeter floodlights blinked on, illuminating the villa and its surrounding grounds in a blinding daylight glow.

Holy shit.

He couldn't believe she'd done it—betrayed his presence to the entire mansion.

Then again, it shouldn't come as much of a surprise. He had certainly earned her scorn. Arabella Genova owed him nothing anymore, not even an explanation for how she'd ended up on the arm—and possibly in the bed—of a criminal scum like Massioni.

No choice, she'd said.

What the hell did she mean by that?

"Bella—" He reached for her, but she jerked out of his grasp, putting several paces between them.

"Get out, Ettore." Her soft brown eyes were desperate beneath her furrowed brows. And outside the closed door of her quarters, it sounded as though several of Massioni's men were already rushing up the stairs to the second floor. She threw an anxious glance over her shoulder at the pounding of approaching feet in the hallway. Her voice was a tight, fearful whisper. "Please, go. Get out of here while you still have a chance!"

Jesus, she was terrified.

And it wasn't directed at him.

What the hell had that bastard done to her?

Savage ground out a curse, feeling precious seconds tick by. He had a mission to carry out tonight—and he would—but not until Bella was safe and secured. Whether or not she intended to cooperate with that plan.

"Come with me." He grabbed for her again, this time snagging her wrist.

"No. Let go of me!" she cried, projecting her voice louder than necessary. For who? Massioni and his goons? "I said stay away from me!"

"Listen to me, damn it." Savage took hold of her shoulders and forced her to meet his gaze. "I'm trying to save you, Bella."

She scoffed brittly. "You can't save me. No one can."

Christ, she really believed that. He knew her too well to think otherwise. He'd always been able to read her emotions in her eyes, in that lovely face that had haunted his dreams for longer than he cared to admit.

When she tried to break loose from his hold, he realized there was only one way he would be able to get her out of the villa without fighting her every step of the way.

She might hate him even more for this, but he had no choice either. He wasn't about to leave her behind.

Laying his palm against her forehead, he tranced her into an immediate and deep sleep.

She no sooner sagged into his arms than the door to her quarters burst open and two armed guards filled the space.

Savage was crouched low, having just guided Bella's limp body to rest on the rug. His weapon was already drawn and ready as the pair of Breed males crashed into the room. He dropped them both with sniper precision, squeezing off two headshots that nailed each guard between the eyes.

There would be more behind them. By the sound of the chaos unraveling all around the villa now, Savage expected he'd have to take on Massioni's entire army of thugs as soon as he stepped out of the room.

Fortunately, he had another plan.

Lifting Bella over his shoulder in a fireman's carry, he dashed to the other side of her suite where a large window overlooked the circular driveway below. A handful of armed guards scurried across the cobbled bricks, some heading into the mansion as backup while others fanned out to patrol the surrounding grounds.

The odds of getting past the security detail down there weren't great, but they were a hell of a lot better than charging into the fray inside the villa.

Lifting the glass with a mental command, he swung his legs over the sill, then dropped to the ground with Bella held securely in his arms.

He threw another psychic order at the nearest vehicle, smiling to himself when the V12 engine of the blue Pagani rumbled to life. The gullwing doors lifted and Savage hurried over to slip Bella into the passenger seat and fasten her in.

One of the perimeter patrol guards spotted him and shouted the alarm to the others. Bullets rang out from all directions. Savage dodged the incoming fire, diving into the driver's seat of the sleek sports car and dropping the doors. Throwing the vehicle into gear, he sped away from the villa just as Massioni and several of his lieutenants came pouring out behind him.

Savage already had the detonator in hand, the safety switched off.

He pushed the trigger on it, watching in the rearview mirror as a sudden fireball ignited and the whole place exploded against the night sky. The percussion made the Pagani jump on the pavement, but he held the wheel and pushed the pedal to the floor.

He couldn't deny his satisfaction at seeing the fiery plume and cloud of black, roiling smoke behind him. He only hoped the explosives did the job as intended. Ordinarily, he'd stick around to make sure his target was neutralized, but not tonight.

Not with precious cargo in tow.

His gaze strayed to Bella. Slumped in her red silk gown on the seat beside him, she slept as peacefully as a kitten, her mind still caught in the web of the trance he'd placed on her. The urge to touch her was too much to resist. Reaching over, he smoothed an errant blonde tendril from her cheek.

Damn, she was even lovelier than he recalled. No longer the coltish Breedmate girl who'd been his best friend's sister. No longer the tomboy teenager who used to delight in racing through the cultivated fields of her family's vineyard, but a twenty-eight-year-old woman with a refined beauty that stirred everything male in him.

Not to mention his blood.

Memories of a night ten years ago came to life in his mind in vivid, erotic detail. Her warm, naked skin against his. Her sweet, breathless cries as he tasted every virgin inch of her beautiful body.

Her trusting, open-hearted gaze as he made love to her for the first—and only—time.

How she must have hated him...after.

He'd despised himself enough for both of them. If he'd been in the least to blame for pushing Bella toward another man—especially one like Vito Massioni—he would never forgive himself.

And if he wanted to pretend he had forgotten her even for a moment during the past decade, seeing her beside him now was as if all that time had simply evaporated.

He didn't know what he was going to do with her now. She sure as fuck hadn't been part of the equation when he'd set out on tonight's mission, but seeing her again had changed everything. Once he had spotted her inside the villa, nothing would have kept him from making sure she was safe.

Not even Bella herself could have stopped him.

So much for a simple operation going according to plan.

Savage forced his gaze away from her and put both hands back on the wheel. His eyes trained on the road, he buried the Pagani's accelerator and headed for the highway that would take them back to Rome.

Chapter 4

Bella couldn't wake from the sleep that cocooned her.

Nor did she want to.

Warm fingers stroked the side of her face as she slept, soothing her with a touch that was both sheltering and enticing. So strong. So infinitely gentle.

Ettore's touch.

Her senses knew it, even if her mind struggled to comprehend. His caress felt like a dream, but it was real. As real as he was, seated close enough to her that his scent filled her lungs with each waking breath she drew.

No, this was no dream.

This was something deeper than sleep.

Her head felt thick, as if her mind were cushioned in cotton.

Then she remembered. The shock of seeing Ettore inside Massioni's villa. Her dread at learning what he had come there to do.

She remembered him insisting that she leave with him, go somewhere safe. When she refused, he had reached up to touch her brow...

He'd tranced her!

Outrage speared through her. The sudden jolt of adrenaline and fury helped shake off the loose threads of the fading trance. She opened her eyes and found Ettore glancing at her. His handsome face and solemn hazel eyes held her gaze in the dim light of the vehicle's dashboard.

Beneath her, the low purr of an engine vibrated.

"Are you okay?" he asked, drawing his hand away from her face now.

She instantly missed the warmth, despite the alarm that was flooding her veins.

"What are you doing?" She dragged herself out of her slump in the soft leather seat. On the other side of the passenger window, the nighttime landscape was a blur. Jesus, Ettore was driving like a bat out of hell. She swung an anxious look behind them. "Where's Massioni?"

"Don't worry about him. He was mine to deal with. And I did."

Fresh horror swamped her. "You killed him?"

Ettore looked at her, his expression grim. "I hope so, but there wasn't time to verify that."

Oh, God. No. "Where are we going?"

A frown creased his brow. "I'm taking you to Rome, Bella. You'll be safest at the Order's command center there. My comrades and I will make sure of that."

The Order. As shocked as she was to realize the golden, charming young man she had known all those years ago now made his living dealing in violence and death as a member of that lethal organization, she also knew that no one—not even the Order—could protect her from the worst of Vito Massioni's threats.

For all she knew, it was already too late.

"Let me out of here, Ettore. Let me out right now."

"What do you mean, let you out?" He gaped at her as if she had lost her mind. "Sweetheart, we're going a hundred and twenty miles an hour."

"I have to go back. Please, Ettore!"

Overcome with worry, she fumbled with her seatbelt, unfastening it and tearing it away from her body. She had to get out of the car and go back to beg Massioni's forgiveness.

If he was still alive.

Dear God, don't let him be dead.

Don't let her family be killed because of her failure to protect them.

A sob raked her throat. "Goddammit, I said stop this fucking car!"

He slowed the growling sports car and eased off the empty highway to the shoulder. As soon as the vehicle stopped, she leaped out. She paused only long enough to toss her high heels into the grass, then started running the opposite way on the rough gravel that edged the pavement.

Ettore's curse exploded behind her. "What the hell are you doing?"

He caught up to her instantly, gifted with Breed genetics that made him faster than any other creature on the planet. He blocked her path, his big male body filling her vision and all of her senses. When she tried to dodge him, his hands came down firmly on her shoulders, holding her still.

"Talk to me, Arabella. Tell me what this is about."

"My family." She couldn't contain the shiver that rocked her when she thought about what they might be enduring because of her, possibly at this very moment. "Massioni promised me that if anything ever happened to him, he'd have them killed."

Ettore's scowl deepened. "Your father might have something to say about that. Your brother, Consalvo, too."

She gazed up at him, shaking her head in misery. "My father's dead. So is Sal. I guess you didn't know. How would you, right? You left and never looked back."

He flinched as if her words stung as much as a slap. Yet when he spoke, there was only quiet, patient concern in his deep voice. "What happened?"

"It was Sal," she said, still wounded by her brother's fall from grace—and the betrayal that followed. "Three years ago, my father made the mistake of turning over the vineyard to Sal. Things didn't go very well. He was careless with the books. Worse than careless. None of us realized how deeply in debt the business was—or why—until Sal's mate, Chiara, confided in me about his gambling. She was worried for him, and for the future of their infant son. But it was already too late. Sal got mixed up with bad people, the worst of them being Vito Massioni."

Ettore blew out a sharp curse. "The idiot. Sallie owed him money?"

"A lot of money. More than any of us could pay. By the time we learned what he'd done, Massioni was out of patience. He tortured Sal, nearly killed him." Bella took a fortifying breath. "My brother was scared and desperate, in fear for his life. He couldn't have been thinking clearly… At least, that's what I've had to tell myself in order to forgive him for what he did to me."

She watched Ettore's eyes darken with grave understanding. "Your brother is the reason you're with Massioni?"

She nodded. "Vito showed up at our Darkhaven one night, along with a dozen armed men. He wasn't there to negotiate. The men shot my father in front of all of us. Sal was going to be next. He made all kinds of promises, offered to give Massioni the house, the vineyard—everything he could think of. None of it appealed to Vito, of course. He had plenty of property, plenty of money. Then Sal looked at me."

"No." Ettore's voice dropped to a low growl. "Jesus, he didn't."

Bella swallowed. "Sal told him about my gift for scrying. He told Massioni to imagine how much richer he could be if he had the ability to see the future. Sal promised that I was worth ten times as much as the debt he owed. In the end, I'm sure he was right. Massioni took me away that night, after giving his men the order to kill Sal."

Ettore's eyes were no longer dark, but crackling with shards of amber that ignited with his rage. As he spoke, the tips of his fangs glinted bright white behind his lips. "That cowardly son of a bitch. If your brother were alive right now, I'd fucking kill him myself." He reached up to touch her face and she could feel the power of his fury beneath the tenderness of his fingers.

"It doesn't matter anymore. I did what I had to in order to survive. Chiara and my little nephew are what matter most to me. They're the reason I stayed with Massioni. He held their lives ransom to make sure I never crossed him or tried to get away."

"Well, he can't hurt anyone now," Ettore said. "As of tonight, Vito Massioni's either dead or damned close to it."

"No. You don't understand." She stepped back, shaking her head. She wished she could stand there all night under the warmth of his caress, but her dread was only intensifying by the moment. "You don't realize what you've done, Ettore. He gave instructions to his entire criminal network to hunt down Chiara and Pietro if anything ever happened to him. If he's dead, so are they. Or they will be soon."

Ettore studied her for a moment before hissing a tight curse. "Your brother's widow and her boy—are they still at the vineyard?"

She nodded.

"Fuck. That's three hours in the other direction." He stared at her, grim but resolute. "If we push it, the Pagani should get us there in under two."

"Does that mean you'll help me?"

"To my last breath, Arabella." He cupped her face in his strong palm, his eyes blazing with determination and something deeper. Something that lit a dormant hope in her chest and made her veins tingle with heat.

She knew he felt the same kindling of emotion too. It was there in his glittering eyes, and in the lengthening points of his fangs.

He may have abandoned her without explanation a decade ago, but all of the attraction and need that had existed between them was still there. Still burning inside both of them.

"Come on," he said after a long moment, his voice rough. "We'd better go."

Chapter 5

They made it to Potenza in just under two hours, thanks to clear late-night roadways and the seven hundred horses at work inside the Pagani's massive engine.

Savage turned onto a narrow two-lane and headed for the Genova family vineyard even before Bella pointed to give him directions. He had been born in the same southern province of Italy, and, like her, he had spent the better part of his youth traipsing around the volcanic soil foothills of the region's imposing Mount Vulture.

Unlike Bella, however, he had no family of his own. Whoever his parents were, they'd been gone from his life soon after he was born. Abandoned when he was just a baby, he'd been raised in one Darkhaven orphanage after another until he was old enough to take care of himself.

He thought he'd found something close to family when he met Bella's brother, Consalvo, at university and the two became fast friends. He had regarded Sal like a brother, helped work the vineyard with the family as if it was his own.

For a long time, he had actually believed he'd found someplace to belong.

He *had* belonged...until his desire for Arabella had been found out and he'd been informed by her father that he was no longer welcome there.

Not good enough for his daughter.

Bella deserved something better.

Hell, Savage wouldn't argue that, even now.

But as he glanced over at her and watched her lovely face turn ashen with dread on their approach to the long gravel drive that led to the homestead at the base of the mountain, he felt a wave of possessiveness—and protectiveness—he could not deny.

And he felt guilt too.

For leaving her the way he had, for letting her think he didn't care.

For not being present to ensure that she never knew a moment of pain or heartache or fear.

All the things he could see playing across her features now.

Because of him.

She sucked in a sharp breath when she spotted the ominous-looking, empty black sedan parked halfway up the drive to the rambling villa. "Oh, no. Ettore, we're too late."

He clamped his molars tight, holding back the curse that leaped to his tongue. She was right. It didn't look good.

A plan formed in his head—a risky one, but the best option he had.

He didn't dare ditch the car with Bella inside it, and damned if he was going to let her out of his sight for as much as a second.

"Slide down as far as you can," he told her. "Don't move, Bella. Not unless I tell you to."

She shot him an anxious glance but did as he instructed.

He swept off his black knit skullcap and tossed it aside. Instead of keeping his cautious pace up the meandering drive, Savage gunned the engine, letting the tires chew up the dirt and dust as he roared all the way to the homestead.

Up ahead in the dark, a pair of Breed thugs in black suits were prowling the perimeter of the house and surrounding grounds. Shit. They were both carrying semiautomatic pistols and looking short on patience. Maybe that was a good thing where Bella's family members were concerned.

Savage threw the Pagani into park but left the engine running. Since his attire could raise questions he didn't want to answer, he would have to employ his unique brand of obfuscation in order to get him past the other males' suspicion.

Using the Breed ability that served him well in his stealth line of work, he conjured an illusion that turned his tactical gear into a black suit and altered his face and hair color. Then he pulled his own semiauto 9mm and climbed out of the car as if he had every right to be there.

"Jesus Christ," he muttered loudly as he stalked toward the goateed man out front. "Where the fuck are the other guys?"

The henchman scowled. "What other guys? Far as I know, me and Luigi were the only ones called out for this job. Who the hell are you?"

"Backup," Savage said, giving the man a look of disdain. He called out to the second man, a thick-necked mountain of a male who was just coming around from the rear of the farmhouse. "What the fuck's taking you so long, Luigi? You find that bitch and her brat back there?"

Luigi shook his head as he started jogging over to meet them. "Not yet. They must've cleared out before we got here."

Savage grunted. "Good."

He popped a round into each man's skull before either of them could react. The two would-be killers dead on the ground, he jogged back to the Pagani. Arabella was still hunkered down on the floor in front of the passenger seat like he'd instructed her. Good girl.

He opened the door. "It's okay. Chiara and your nephew aren't here and the two men sent to find them won't be looking for them anymore."

"Thank God." She lifted her head, pushing herself up to peer into the darkness where Massioni's men lay unmoving in the grass near the house. "But Chiara wouldn't have known to run away. There wouldn't have been time to get very far, especially with a three-year-old in tow." She glanced up at him, worry—and a small glimmer of hope—in her soft brown eyes. "But I think I might know where they are."

Savage held out his hand to assist her from the car. Gathering up the long skirt of her dress, she ran past the dead Breed males with Savage at her side. They entered the sacked villa and she headed immediately for the sampling room at the back of the expansive house. An immense wine cellar was attached to the room, its floor-to-ceiling wine racks filled with bottles of nearly every vintage the vineyard had ever produced.

"Over here," Bella said, walking to the far wall.

The bottles housed in those racks looked to be the oldest in the collection. Most of them were covered in a fine layer of dust. Pulling a sliding wooden ladder toward her, she climbed up and reached for one of the highest bottles in the old rack. Instead of pulling the aged bottle of Aglianico out, she twisted it clockwise.

It wasn't a bottle. It was a lever to a secret chamber.

One narrow section of racked wine popped open soundlessly.

Bella swung a glance over her shoulder at him. "My father had this panic room installed during the wars after First Dawn twenty years ago."

She started to duck inside. Savage caught her by the arm. "Stay close to me, Bella. If anything happens to you, I couldn't…"

He let the thought trail, but his touch lingered longer than necessary. She gave him a curious look, then nodded.

They stepped inside the unlit, cavernous room. Large oak barrels, shelves of paper supplies, and chunky, hand-hewn wooden tables made the secret chamber appear to be nothing more remarkable than a workroom for the vineyard.

Bella reached to turn on a light switch just inside. "Chiara?" she called softly. "Are you in here? It's me, Arabella."

A small whimper sounded from somewhere behind the barrels. Then a petite, pretty brunette emerged from the shadows, her dark-haired toddler son held protectively in her arms. "Bella!"

The two women raced to each other, embracing amid Chiara's tears and Bella's quiet assurances that she and Pietro were okay now. That they were safe.

Savage stood back from the emotional reunion, all too conscious of the fact that every minute they delayed here was one more minute they risked being discovered. They were fortunate that only two of Massioni's henchmen had been dispatched to the vineyard. That didn't mean there wouldn't be more sent to sniff around and make sure the job was finished.

The dead Breed males in the yard would be ashed by the morning sun, but whoever sent them would be waiting for them to return or report in.

And now that he was thinking about daylight...

It was late, and all too soon it would be dawn. They were too far afield to make the drive back to the command center before the sun rose and ashed him, too, which meant he needed to find them somewhere secure to settle in for the night.

Grabbing his phone, Savage called the scrambled line at the Order in Rome to apprise them of the situation. He'd already ignored more than one call from base demanding the status of the mission. He'd have hell to pay when he got back, no doubt. Probably right now too.

Trygg's dark growl greeted him on the other end. "Having a good time out there?"

Savage grunted. "There's been a slight change of plans."

"No shit? Was that before or after you jeopardized the entire mission in order to chase after some former tail?"

Okay, so maybe he deserved that. He definitely deserved it. But Trygg didn't understand, and Savage didn't have time to explain it right now. "Her name's Arabella Genova. I had to go back in for her and get her out of there. You're going to have to trust me on that."

"Not my trust you need to worry about," Trygg said. "Commander Archer's on a call with Lucan Thorne in D.C. as we speak. They weren't happy to hear you went AWOL in the middle of an op."

"Yeah, well, I got the job done."

"You sure about that? You verified Massioni blew up with his villa, right?" When Savage let the question hang a second too long, Trygg hissed a low curse. "You didn't verify. Jesus, Savage. I hope to fuck she's worth it, man."

He glanced over at Bella. Yeah, she was worth it. Her life—the relief and happiness he saw in her face right now—was worth everything.

"If I fucked up with Massioni, I'll handle it. Right now, I need to find a safe house for the day. I've got two Breedmates and a three-year-old Breed male with me here in Potenza right now. I need to make sure they're somewhere secure."

"Two females and a kid? I'm not gonna ask," Trygg muttered. He went silent for a moment, then heaved a surly sigh. "How far are you from Matera?"

Savage knew the town, had prowled the ancient streets and subterranean caverns of the old settlement more than a few times in his youth. "It's not far. An hour, give or take."

"Get there. I know somewhere you can go." Trygg gave him quick instructions, landmarks to guide him to where he needed to go once he arrived. From the sound of it, his comrade wasn't sending him into the touristy heart of the historic town, but down into the Paleolithic *sassi*—the neighborhood of ancient limestone caves that clung to the steep walls of Matera's central ravine. "Take the old stone steps behind the church. Follow the path on the left. Someone will be waiting to meet you and take you to a safe shelter."

"Who am I looking for?"

"A Breed male with long black hair and obsidian eyes. His name is Scythe."

"Scythe? Sounds like a real hospitable guy."

"You didn't ask for hospitable. You asked for someplace secure, and that's where I'm sending you."

"Point taken," Savage drawled, reminded that Trygg was nothing if not literal. The deadly, unsociable male dealt in absolutes, whether it came to combat or conversation. "What I'm saying is, you're sure about this male, this Scythe?"

"Completely."

"Care to elaborate?"

There was a long silence, then Trygg finally said, "He's my brother."

Chapter 6

Bella hated to let go of Chiara and Pietro, but Ettore's grave look as he ended his call to the Order left no question that they weren't totally out of danger yet.

"Come on," he said, walking over to collect them. "We can't delay here much longer. It's best if we get moving."

"Back to Rome?"

"There isn't time for that now. It'll be daylight in a few hours. My driving skills tend to suffer when I'm crispy."

She smiled wanly, but it was hard to find any humor in the risks he was taking for her tonight. For all of them now. And she could tell from the tone of his voice that the urgency to move on wasn't motivated only by his Breed aversion to ultraviolet rays. His concern went deeper than that.

"You think he's still alive, don't you?"

A tendon pulsed in Ettore's square jaw. "If he's not dead, I promise you I won't rest until he is. But first I need to make sure you and your family are somewhere secure. My comrade in Rome is arranging for someone to meet us in Matera. We'll have shelter there for as long as we need it."

As Bella and Ettore spoke, Chiara stepped forward with her young son clutching her hand.

Ettore glanced at the boy who was looking up at him warily. He crouched down to his level and placed his hand lightly on the child's shoulder. "You were very brave, keeping your mother safe in here until we arrived. Good work, Pietro."

He nodded shyly at the praise, and Bella's heart squeezed to see the little boy's fear melt away under Ettore's gentle treatment of him.

"How long will we need to stay away?" Chiara asked hesitantly.

Ettore's gaze met Bella's as he stood up. She knew that heavy look, what it meant. The two killers who'd shown up tonight hadn't succeeded, thanks to him, but it was almost certain there would be more behind them. The old vineyard and the rambling house where Bella was raised might never be safe again. Then again, it hadn't truly been safe in years. Not since Massioni entered their lives.

Combing her fingers gently through her little nephew's dark hair, Bella met Chiara's gaze. "We'll figure all of that out later. Right now, we need to do what Ettore says, okay?"

"Yes, of course. May I gather a few things for Pietro before we go? I promise I'll hurry."

Ettore nodded and Bella glanced down at her red gown and bare feet. "I don't suppose you have anything in your closet that would fit me, do you?"

Chiara smiled warmly. "You can look for something in your own closet, *sorella*. I kept your room just as it was on the day you were taken, in the hopes that you would come home again one day."

The kindness of that gesture—the sisterly love from her brother's widow—put a lump in Bella's throat. "Thank you."

She pulled Chiara into a brief hug before Ettore brought them all out of the panic room and back into the empty villa to prepare to leave.

A few minutes later, Bella was dressed in a pair of dark jeans and flats and a black T-shirt. Chiari held Pietro in one arm, a small bag containing his favorite blanket and toys and sundry other necessities slung over her other arm. Ettore took the bag from her and headed outside, leading the way.

"We have to leave the Pagani," he said, bypassing the two-seater sports car. "There's not enough room in it, but we also need to avoid drawing attention. I don't like the idea of taking Massioni's men's vehicle, but I can ditch it after we get to Matera in case anyone's looking for it."

"I've got a truck out back," Chiara said. She pointed to the barn behind the house. "It's not fast, but it'll get us where we're going. And it's plain enough that it won't turn any heads along the way."

Ettore considered for a moment, then shrugged. "Sounds better than our other options."

They retrieved the rust-spotted old pickup truck and climbed in, Bella sandwiched on the narrow bench seat between Ettore and Chiara and Pietro.

It was impossible to ignore the heat of Ettore's thigh pressed against hers as they drove off into the thinning darkness. Being this close to him again, her senses overwhelmed with the warmth and strength and scent of him, Bella knew a contentment—a feeling of security—that had eluded her for so long she hadn't recalled what it was like to feel safe and protected.

She hardly realized how badly she'd craved that feeling until now. With him.

Chiara and Pietro must have felt some degree of safety now too. They had both dozed off just a few minutes into the drive. No doubt the late hour and the stress of what they'd endured tonight had left them exhausted, but Bella knew their peaceful breathing had much to do with the man who'd surely saved their lives.

Bella glanced at Ettore in the soft light of the old truck's dashboard. His eyes were fixed on the open road, one hand slung over the top of the steering wheel. He seemed deep in his own thoughts until the weight of her gaze drew his attention. He looked her way, and although she was embarrassed to be caught staring at him, she couldn't pretend she hadn't been.

"Thank you for helping them," she said quietly. "Thank you for helping all of us tonight."

He gave a small shake of his head. "There's no need to thank me, Bella. I would do anything for you. Don't you know that?"

No, she didn't know that. For all she knew, she'd meant absolutely nothing to him. Not ten years ago. Certainly not all this time later. "Why did you do it, Ettore? Why did you leave and never come back? Was it because of something I did?"

"No." His answer came swiftly, his brows furrowing in a scowl. "Christ, no. You didn't do anything at all. Tell me that's not what they let you believe..."

"They?" A sick feeling opened up in the pit of her stomach. "You mean my family? You mean my father and Sal?"

His silent stare was confirmation enough.

"Tell me," she prompted. "What did they do?"

He glanced back at the road. "They were only looking out for your best interests, Bella. They noticed we were growing closer—they noticed my interest in you as a woman—and your father wasn't pleased. Neither was Sal, actually."

"Are you saying they pushed you away? No... Surely they would not. Are you saying they didn't want us together, so they forced us apart?"

Anger clawed up the back of her throat. She could hardly stand the thought of what their interference had caused her. To think she had wept over her father's murder. To think she had wept for Sal, even after he'd betrayed her to Vito Massioni.

But selling her out to that criminal thug hurt less than knowing the two men she trusted the most all her life had actually betrayed her even more egregiously long before then, when they stole her chance at a future with Ettore.

He slanted her a sober look. "They loved you, Arabella. Your father wanted to make sure you found a male who could provide for you, give you all the things you deserved in life. Your father and Sal both wanted only what was best for you."

Her answering scoff was brittle. "Look how that turned out."

"They couldn't have known how things would end up," he gently assured her. "But I wish I had known. I wish the Order had been on to Vito Massioni years ago, so I could've killed the bastard before he had the chance to lay a hand on you."

"It could've been worse," she admitted quietly. "I endured his temper sometimes, but at least I avoided his lust."

When Ettore glanced at her, there was surprise in his gaze, and more than a little relief. "You mean, he never—"

"Never," she said. "I told him my gift for scrying would only last as long as I was a virgin. Since I made him wealthy with my visions, he apparently decided he enjoyed collecting his money more than he would enjoy abusing me."

He smirked. "Clever girl. Except for one thing."

She felt a blush creep over her cheeks at the reminder.

She wasn't a virgin. She had given that part of her to Ettore. It had been their one and only time together.

The next night, he was gone.

"Fortunately, Massioni never doubted me. I think he might've eventually, but he had other women to slake his needs."

"Thank God," Ettore muttered. He frowned, his hazel gaze turbulent with stifled fury. "What about your visions, Bella? Did you never see any hint of your brother's troubles in your scrying bowl?"

She shook her head. "I don't see visions that relate to myself or the people I care for. My ability has never worked like that."

Which was why she'd never seen Ettore either, although it hadn't stopped her from trying to find him with her gift over the years he'd been gone. But her scrying had never found him.

Not even as he'd planned for and carried out his attack on Vito Massioni.

She dearly hoped Ettore had been successful, because if Massioni were alive to get his hands on her now, his punishment would be beyond brutal.

Ettore's mouth flattened into a grim line. "I never should've agreed to leave, no matter what your family wanted. It wasn't their decision to make. I didn't understand that until after I was gone." He reached over and stroked her cheek. "I should've come back for you,

Bella. I'm sorry I wasn't there."

She turned into his caress, feeling no animosity toward him, only gratitude. And an affection that went far deeper than that.

Far deeper than the desire she felt simply for being seated so closely beside him, his comforting touch lingering against her face.

"You're here now," she said, pressing a soft kiss to the center of his palm.

His eyes flickered with sparks of amber light as her lips met his skin. She only meant the contact to be one of gratefulness and caring, but she felt the jolt of awareness too.

Her chest tightened, heat spreading across her breasts, licking down to her core.

Oh, yes, she still cared for him.

She wanted him.

Memories of stolen kisses and secret, tender embraces filled her head. She'd had only one night with Ettore, naked in each other's arms, but she had held it close to her heart ever since.

Neither the cruelty of time nor fate had diminished anything she felt for him. To the contrary, it had only made the craving deepen. It had only made her recognize how keenly she had felt his loss all this time.

And how profoundly happy she was to be reunited with him now.

Even if in a shadowed corner of her heart she dreaded that fate wasn't nearly finished with them yet.

Chapter 7

Savage didn't know how he'd managed to endure more than an hour in the truck, seated so close to Bella. Her thigh had rested against his the whole trip, contact that had distracted him, soothed him...aroused him beyond reason.

It sent his mind spinning back in time, to another evening drive they'd taken together on vineyard business. The one that had ended with both of them undressed and tangled together on a blanket under a midnight blue sky streaked with shooting stars.

"Come on, Ettore! Isn't it amazing?"

She grabbed a bottle of the newest Aglianico from the wooden cases in back of the truck and started running up the side of the nearby hill. He watched her go, her long legs bare and her curvy backside clad in grape-stained, faded denim shorts. He was always in a state of arousal around her, but seeing her dance away from him under the thin moon glow turned his cock to granite.

"Bella, you'd better come back. I don't think this is a good idea." *Nevertheless, he pulled an old wool blanket from behind the seat and jogged after her.*

She helped him spread it out on the cool grass, then pulled him down next to her. "Here, open this." She handed him the bottle and a corkscrew.

"I don't drink wine," he reminded her as he pulled the cork out with a soft pop. None of his kind did, but she knew that well enough.

"Do you ever wish you could? Even a taste?"

"No." He had never craved wine, but then he watched her tip the bottle to her lips to take a sip and he knew a thirst unlike any he'd ever known. Her throat worked as she swallowed, her head tipped back, drawing his eyes to the creamy column of her neck.

He cleared his throat, searching for his voice as his fangs punched out of his gums and his vision began to fire with amber. "Your father and Sal are expecting us back at the vineyard."

She slowly brought the bottle down from her mouth and set it in the grass. Her lips were wet, as dark as cherries from the wine. Long black lashes framed the solemn pools of her eyes. "Do you want to go, Ettore?"

He knew it as the chance it was—his only hope to stop this need for Bella before it went too far. They had been circling this moment for weeks. Hell, from the moment he first walked on to the Genova property.

Fleeting glances. Brief touches. Shared laughter. Then, later, after he'd fought his attraction for as long as he could, there had been a kiss, a few stolen embraces. Followed by heated caresses that had left both of them in flames.

But she was an innocent, just eighteen years old to his twenty-five.

Even worse, she was the Breedmate sister of his closest friend.

The last thing he should be doing was sitting beside her in the starlight, staring at her throat and wishing he was a better man. One with honor enough to lie and say he wasn't out of his mind with desire for her.

"What do you want, Ettore?"

"You."

He took her down beneath him on the blanket and unwrapped her as reverently as a precious gift. Each breathless moment was seared into his senses, from her soft moans as he kissed and licked and sucked every tempting inch of her...to her shuddering cries as he entered her virgin body and introduced her to an even deeper pleasure as the sea of shooting stars skated overhead.

Savage groaned at the uninvited recollection and the need it stoked in him even now.

By the time they reached the ancient hillside town of Matera, his body was rife with desire, his cock so hard it was a wonder he'd been able to drive.

His palm still burned from the sweet kiss she'd placed there.

His veins throbbed with hunger for her—a hunger that was startlingly more intense than simple desire. If he'd imagined that their years apart would cool his feelings for her, that tender kiss to the center of his hand had obliterated all hope of that.

Holy hell, he was in trouble here.

He should be thinking about his duty to the Order—and about the mission status that was uncertain at best—yet his mind was wrapped around Arabella Genova.

So was his heart. Although to be fair, that part of him had been hers for a lot longer than his life had been pledged to the Order.

How many times had he considered defying the wishes of her father and brother to go back and beg for her forgiveness and take her away with him forever? How many human blood Hosts had he drunk from, wishing it was Bella's vein that was nourishing him instead, her Breedmate blood ensuring that she would always be his?

Now, all he had were regrets.

He only hoped he could somehow get the chance to make things right. But first he needed to make sure she was safe.

"This way," he told the women, after leaving the old truck in a church parking lot as Trygg had instructed.

Carrying Chiara's bag so she could focus on her child, Savage placed his hand at the small of Bella's back and brought them to a flight of well-worn stone steps on the other side of the church. The stairs descended away from the quaint hotels and restaurants near Matera's city center, into the thickly settled community of limestone dwellings that appeared to grow out of the walls of the broad ravine.

Waning blue moonlight and the golden glow of random lanterns and street lamps illuminated the uneven trail Trygg had given them to follow. At the predawn hour, there were no tourists on the tangled network of stone paths and meandering steps of the *sassi*. The ravine was quiet, nothing but the sound of their footsteps on the dusty old cobbles and the occasional jangle of a sheep's bell from the flock starting to awaken on a grassy flat across the way.

Savage followed the path to the left, as he'd been told, which took them toward what appeared to be the low-rent section of the Paleolithic-era neighborhood. White limestone residences with the occasional flower box in their window or potted plant outside the door gave way to an unlit stretch of cobbles lined with rustic domiciles in various states of neglect, most with weeds and cactus sprouting out of their cracked and crumbling walls.

"Stay close," Savage advised the women as he led them deeper into the settlement. "We should almost be there now."

A few minutes later, just as Trygg had described, his brother waited up ahead on the walkway. At least, Savage hoped the immense, black-haired Breed male was Scythe.

As they approached, Savage walking protectively in front of Bella and Chiara, the other male lifted his head and swung a glance in their direction. Long ebony hair hung several inches past his shoulders, and a trimmed black beard outlined the grave set of his mouth. The male's eyes, as dark as jet, narrowed on Savage across the distance.

Yep. Definitely Scythe.

Savage nodded to him in greeting. Scythe's face remained expressionless within his curtain of dark hair. Dressed in a black leather trench coat that covered more black clothing beneath it, the male looked every bit a cold-blooded killer.

Which was saying something, coming from Savage, a warrior whose stock-in-trade was dealing death.

At Savage's back, he heard Bella suck in a shallow gasp.

"It's all right," he told her, touching her arm in reassurance. "This is who we're supposed to meet."

Without introduction, Scythe turned and started walking away. Apparently, he was as people-friendly as his brother. So long as the male was trustworthy and his safe house was secure, Savage would give the lack of social skills a pass.

"Let's go," he said, pausing to press a kiss to Bella's forehead. "We'll be safe here, I promise."

They followed Scythe to one of the last cave houses on the path, a squatty residence devoid of windows and accessible through a door that was reinforced with an iron grate. Savage wasn't expecting much as the other Breed male opened the door and let them inside, but it turned out the place only appeared forbidding and neglected from the outside. They stepped into a comfortable, if minimalist, dwelling with hand-hewn furnishings, arched stone ceilings, and warm, rug-covered floors.

Once they were inside, Scythe motioned for them to follow him farther into the place. More rooms were burrowed out of the rock of the ravine, connected by snaking tunnels large enough for both Breed males to walk through at their full height.

"I don't generally have guests," Scythe announced, sounding none too pleased. His voice was low and dark, almost a snarl as he strode ahead of them, his words echoing off the walls. "There is a small bed in the chamber to your right, and a larger one in the room at the end of this corridor. Make use of them as you wish."

Savage glanced at Bella. "You and Chiara take the beds. I don't need to sleep."

It was true enough. As Breed, he didn't require a lot of rest, but he doubted his thoughts would give him much peace anyway. To say nothing of his body, which was still thrumming with want of Bella.

She looked as if she meant to protest his sacrifice, but her sister-in-law was teetering on her feet and Pietro hadn't lifted his head since they left the truck. "I'll go help them settle in."

Savage remained in the passage as the women departed for the room. When he glanced at Scythe, he found the male watching Chiara through narrowed eyes. A dark scowl creased his brow.

"Trygg didn't say anything about a child being in danger."

"He didn't?" Savage frowned. "I'm sure I mentioned the boy when I spoke with him."

Scythe grunted. "Yeah. I'm sure you did too."

The cryptic response intrigued him. "Is it a problem?"

Scythe didn't answer, which told Savage far more than any words ever could. "If you or the females need anything, let me know."

Okay, conversation over apparently. Savage held out his hand to the other male. "Thank you. I owe you for this, and I won't forget it."

Scythe stared at his outstretched hand for a long moment. At first, Savage didn't understand why. Then he saw it—the severed stump at the end of the other male's right wrist where there had once been a hand.

And there was something else unusual about Scythe that he'd missed until now as well.

Around his *dermaglyph*-covered neck was a circle of mangled, vicious looking scars. By the severity of them, Savage had to guess that the Breed male had nearly lost his head at some point in his life too.

Since Breed genetics could heal all but the most catastrophic of injuries, Scythe must have been starving for blood or already half-dead from some other cause at the time this wound was inflicted.

Scythe shrugged. "We'd been raised to think we were invincible. It made many of us reckless. Not many survived after we got our first taste of freedom."

"Freedom from what?"

"From our collars."

The newsflash took Savage completely by surprise. He gaped at the obviously lethal, clearly antisocial Breed male. "Are you telling me that you were born a Hunter?"

Looking at him now, it made sense. As far as assassins and stealth operatives went, they didn't come any deadlier than the Hunters—first generation Breed males who'd been bred off the same Ancient sire and raised to be merciless killers by the Order's chief adversary. To keep his scattered army of perfect assassins obedient, Dragos had outfitted each of them with an ultraviolet collar that discouraged defiance or escape. Punishment was instant and final.

Dragos's secret program had been in operation for decades before he was taken out by Lucan and his warriors twenty years ago.

As for the Hunters themselves, they were all but legend among the Breed now, with only a handful known to exist.

Evidently, Savage was looking at one of them.

He met Scythe's shark-black stare in question. "Trygg said you were his brother."

"He is. As are the others."

"Others?"

Scythe acknowledged with a curt nod. "The other lost boys. The dozens of young Hunters who escaped their collars when Dragos was killed."

Chapter 8

Ettore and their intimidating host were just parting ways as Bella stepped out of the bedroom where Chiara was resting with Pietro. She hesitated until the immense black-haired male had walked off before she approached.

Ettore glanced her way, a look of lingering astonishment in his eyes.

"Is everything all right with your friend?" she asked.

He grunted, raking a hand through his loose blond waves. "I wouldn't exactly call Scythe a friend just yet, but yeah, we're good."

Bella registered the name with an inward shudder. It was certainly a fitting moniker for the curt, menacing-looking Breed male. "If Scythe's glower is anything to go by, he doesn't seem happy to be saddled with houseguests."

"Are you kidding? That is his happy face." Ettore's grin flashed, revealing the twin dimples that had never failed to charm her. "How are Chiara and Pietro?"

"Exhausted. They're already asleep."

"You should be too," he said, his voice dropping to a tone of tender concern. His hand rested warmly on her shoulder. "Come on. Let's get you settled in the other bedroom."

It all seemed so surreal, being in this strange place, feeling safe despite the fact that she was on the run from an evil man and his network of criminal associates.

Ettore did that for her. She had always felt safe when she was with him. The guns and blades bristling from the belt that circled his waist had nothing to do with how protected he made her feel. It was him, the man, who had always been able to put her at ease.

As much as he aroused her.

Her skin still felt too warm, too tight, as they paused together at the chamber's open doorway. Everything they'd said in the truck, the stolen caresses they'd shared in those brief moments of semiprivacy earlier tonight, now hung between them like a wound that needed tending.

Ettore seemed to feel the same awareness that she did. The heat radiating from him was palpable, his touch at the small of her back light, yet searing. She wanted to feel his hands on her everywhere, not just in comfort or reassurance, but in passion.

He cursed as his eyes met hers, his hazel irises dark but glittering with flecks of amber. "For God's sake, don't look at me like that, sweetheart. I'm hanging by a thread here."

"I am too." She couldn't resist reaching up to him, letting her hands skim the firm muscles of his chest. "I've been hanging by a thread since you showed up at our vineyard with my brother all those years ago, Ettore."

His heart was thundering. His pulse slammed against her palm, hammering like a drum. He searched her gaze for a long moment, his breath rolling in deep, panting gusts.

The curse that boiled out of him was sharp, hissed between his teeth and fangs. "I wasn't expecting any of this. My first duty is to the Order. I have a mission to carry out. Until I'm certain I've completed it, I shouldn't be thinking about anything else. Not even you. Hell, especially not you."

"Of course. I understand." She glanced away, weathering a sting she hadn't seen coming. "Ettore, I didn't mean to suggest—"

He took her hand and hauled her against him, silencing her with a kiss. When he drew back from her lips, his gaze had gone molten.

"I have no right to be thinking about anything but my duty to the Order. That's what I keep telling myself, Arabella. But then I look at you and none of those other things matter."

She swallowed, watching the fire dance in his eyes. His pupils were narrowed to thin black slits, and his fangs surged even larger behind his parted lips. The sight of his transformation sped her pulse, while at her hip, the hard steel of his arousal sent a current of hot need licking through her senses and straight into her core.

"I walked away once," he snarled. "God help us both, I don't think I can ever do it again."

His name was a jagged sigh on her lips as he grasped her face in his palms and covered her mouth with his once more. Kissing her so deeply she could hardly find her breath, he walked her backward into the chamber with him, kicking the door closed behind them with his boot heel.

Something wild had been unleashed in him. She saw it in his eyes, heard it in the rough scrape of his voice. And now all of that unhinged desire was pouring into her through his kiss.

"You're mine," he murmured against her mouth. Her moan of confirmation evidently wasn't enough. "Say it, Arabella. Let me hear it."

"Yes." Oh, God. She could hardly hold the desire that chased through her. Every hot sweep of his lips over hers, every carnal thrust of his tongue, inflamed a need in her that was swiftly burning out of control. "Please, Ettore. I need you. I need to feel you inside me."

His answer was an animalistic, purely possessive snarl. Pressing her down onto the narrow bed, he stripped away her clothing then quickly removed his own. Part of her wanted him to take things slowly—give her time to savor every nuance of the rock-hard, beautifully formed body she still saw so often in her most fevered dreams.

But the desire they had for each other had been denied for too long.

Too much precious time had been stolen from them already.

She was desperate for him. More than anything, she needed to feel his skin against hers and know that this was no dream now. That he was real. That he was hers again.

Always, she amended silently, allowing the wish to live in her heart as he settled himself atop her.

His eyes blazed as he watched her, his hand moving between their bodies to tease and stroke her sex. His fingers slid through her juices, a groan ripping out of him as he cleaved her folds and found the slick entrance to her body.

"You're already wet for me," he murmured, a grin tilting the edges of his wicked mouth. "Damn, you're soft, Bella. So beautiful. So fucking hot."

She couldn't bite back her whimper of pleasure, both at his praise and at the intensity of her arousal for him. He teased her sensitive flesh, taking her mouth in another deep, soul-searing kiss. She felt him test her tightness with his fingers, starting with one, then adding another, his thumb working a profane magic on her clit.

There had been no one since him, and the euphoria of being naked with him now, in his arms after so much longing, was too much to bear. Her orgasm rushed up on her unexpectedly, far too wild to hold back. She clutched his shoulders as her cry tore out of her throat. Arching off the mattress, she rode the wave to its crest, grinding shamelessly against his hand as the bliss poured over her.

"Open your eyes, baby," he coaxed her as he continued to pleasure her with his fingers. "I've waited too long to see this look on your face again. I swear, Bella, you've only gotten more exquisite."

She caught her lip between her teeth as the aftershocks rippled along her nerve endings, while beneath the pleasure another climax was already beginning to build. "Ettore, please…"

He knew what she needed. Shifting his weight, he positioned himself between her spread thighs. Her body was more than ready for him, slick and hot and open. Yet it was still a shock to feel the impossible thickness of him as he pushed the head of his cock inside her, then thrust to fill her with the hard length of his shaft.

"Bella," he uttered tightly, "you have to tell me if I'm hurting you."

"No." She shook her head, even as tears welled in her eyes. "Oh, God…it feels so good. I thought I remembered, but this…"

"I know, baby." He started to move within her, rocking slowly at first, each stroke taking him deeper, pushing further inside her, until she wasn't sure where he ended and she began.

"Ah, love," he murmured. "Your body is so tight around me. So damned perfect. I can't—"

His words were lost to the feral groan that ripped out of him. Caging her between his forearms, he drove inside her faster, deeper, untamed in his need. His handsome face contorted with the ferocity of his thrusts, his fangs so enormous they filled his mouth.

Bella's gaze fixed on those diamond-bright points as he crashed against her. She couldn't get enough either. She wanted all of him. Not just this moment and the wish that it might last. She wanted forever with Ettore Selvaggio.

After just one time together and ten long years in between, he was still the only man she craved.

In her heart—to the depths of her soul—she knew he was the only man she would ever love.

Chapter 9

Savage didn't fully understand the depth of his mistake until he was buried within Bella's velvet, wet heat. She moaned and sighed as he rolled his hips against her. Her hands roamed his back, her fingernails skating down the valley of his spine, scoring him as he pushed her toward the peak of her release.

Damn, she was lovely. Sweetly angelic, yet sexy as hell. She always had been, but now there was a strength in her too.

There was a power inside her, one that had been forged in the fire of what she'd endured the past three years. No longer the sheltered innocent, but a resilient woman who knew what she wanted and wasn't afraid to take it.

And, incredibly, what she wanted was him.

Still.

The realization stunned him, humbled him. Made him want to hold her close and never let her go.

One taste of her a decade ago had ruined him for any other woman.

Now, every cell in his body was hammering with the need to make her his alone.

In flesh and vow.

God help him, he wanted to claim her in blood too.

He wanted that with a ferocity he'd never known.

Not true, he corrected. He had wanted Bella as his blood-bonded mate even then. Ten years of absence from her had only solidified that resolve.

He loved her, and blood bond or not, he knew he would destroy any male who thought to take her away from him now.

"You're mine, Bella."

He growled the words as he pumped into her, knowing they sounded more like a demand than pledge.

They were both. They were his purpose for breathing, and he couldn't pretend they were anything less.

Not now.

Not when she was coming apart in his arms, her fingers digging into the muscles of his biceps as she cried his name and shattered with the force of her orgasm. The tight walls of her sex vibrated along his cock, tiny muscles gripping him like a slick fist as wave after wave coursed over her taut body.

He watched her come, trying to slow his own release just so he could revel in the pleasure he was giving her. But his need owned him. This female owned him, and trying to temper what she stirred in him was like trying to cage a wildfire.

He took her mouth in a deep kiss, drinking up her little sighs and moans as her climax began to ebb. When her eyelids slowly lifted, she gave him a blissful smile that he would kill to see on her lips for the rest of his life.

His voice was gruff, raw. "You're mine."

"I always have been," she whispered.

Ah, Christ. That tender admission was more than he could bear.

Pleasure seized him, pushing his hips into a fevered tempo. Each thrust took him deeper, made his hunger for her coil tighter, testing its already razor-thin leash.

Bella moved beneath him, meeting every hard stroke, taking him even deeper as she lifted her hips and wrapped her long legs around him.

Her hands roamed his face and shoulders, caressing him,

worshipping him. The knot of his orgasm gathered at the base of his spine, wringing a sharp groan from between his clenched teeth. Blood pounded in his temples, in his cock…in the deadly lengths of his fangs.

"Oh, God," Bella gasped, tipping her head back as the flush of another release swept over her skin. "Ettore…I can't hold on. You feel too good."

He was beyond words now. He was only instinct and need, pure male. Utterly consumed by the remarkable female in his arms. He responded with a triumphant growl as she cried out beneath him. He couldn't stop his hips from moving, nor his blood from pounding with the overwhelming urge to claim his female in every possible way.

The urge became a mantra as his orgasm sped toward its peak.

He didn't realize he was staring at her throat until he heard Bella's soft voice filter through the haze of his blood-tinged thoughts.

"Yes," she said. "Yes, Ettore. I want it too."

When he met her gaze, he found her brown eyes steady and unafraid.

So full of love, it staggered him.

He knew he should turn away, be the stronger one.

He should give her this choice when they both were clear-headed and fully able to process the ramifications of what a bond would mean. One taste of her blood and he would feel her in his veins for as long as either of them lived. He would know her deepest emotions as his own—every joy and sorrow, every pleasure or pain.

And if she should die before him, he would be cursed to feel that too.

The bond was irreversible.

Unbreakable.

Eternal.

Concepts that had never entered his mind with another woman were all he could think of now that he was here with Arabella.

He loved her.

To his soul, he had loved her all this time. And the part of him that was more than mortal wasn't willing to wait another moment to claim her. That possessive, primal part of him wanted to bind her to him irrevocably.

Forever.

There was no place for logic in it, no room for regret.

There was only need.

Only love.

He roared with the ferocity of everything he felt, and as his release took hold of him, Ettore lowered his mouth to Bella's neck and sank his fangs into her tender flesh.

Chapter 10

If the bliss of making love with him had nearly wrecked her, it was nothing compared to the pleasure she felt at the sudden, sharp penetration of his fangs into her carotid.

Bella gasped at the piercing pain, feeling his bite all the way to her marrow. But that initial jolt gave way to a pleasure that defied description as his lips fastened over her skin and he drew the first sip of blood from her wound. Heat raced through her veins like rivers of quicksilver, all of her senses—every fiber of her being—drawn toward the pulse point that now flowed beneath Ettore's mouth.

Each suckling tug, every erotic sweep of his tongue, confirmed what she had already known.

She was his.

If she hadn't been before, the connection he had just activated between them ensured she always would be. He could never take another as his Breedmate so long as his bond to her was intact. For him, there would only be her.

The joy that understanding gave her was almost too much to bear. It filled her heart, even as it awakened something raw and primal inside her.

"You belong to me now, Ettore." She tunneled her fingers through his hair, holding him to her throat as he drank. "Mine."

He moaned, still rocking atop her, their bodies intimately joined.

His strokes intensified along with the suction of his mouth against her vein. The combined sensations flooded her with desire, stoking her need all over again.

"So good," he murmured, his deep voice as rough as gravel, his breath rushing hot against her throat. She felt his tongue sweep over the twin punctures, sealing them closed.

He lifted his head to watch her now. His eyes were glowing as bright as coals, gazing at her with such a ferocity of emotion it stole her breath. She had never seen his fangs look so sharp and unearthly. She licked her lips, hungry to feel them at her throat again.

Everywhere.

He was ferocious and otherworldly, the most magnificent man she'd ever seen.

His wicked mouth curved as he caressed the side of her face and the tender skin where his bite had been. "I can feel you inside me, Bella. I feel your blood in my own veins, in every cell of my body. And I feel your pleasure. I feel how badly you need me to make you come again."

As if to punctuate, he thrust long and slow and deep, a rumble of satisfaction vibrating through him as she cried out in helpless ecstasy.

"My sweet Bella," he said, lowering his head to kiss her forehead, her cheek, her parted lips as she sighed. "I wish you could feel how much I love you."

"Show me," she whispered, reaching up to trace her fingers along his rigid jaw, her gaze drifting to his fangs. "Let me taste you now, Ettore. Give me your bond."

She didn't have to ask him twice.

On a snarl, he brought his wrist up to his mouth and bit into it. Blood dripped onto her breasts, hot splashes of crimson that inflamed her dark thirst for him as he guided her mouth to his wounds.

She sealed her lips over the punctures. The first drop of blood on her tongue felt like a kiss of flame. She moaned, both in shock and in thirst.

She lapped at his skin, astonished at the intense rush of heat through her body as she drank from him. Ettore's blood felt alive with a wildness and strength she could barely comprehend. As powerful as an electric charge, each sip blasted into her body, into her cells…into her soul.

There was no fear left in her. No doubt. Everything peeled away, leaving only their love. This connection that nothing, and no one, could sever.

And beneath the contentment she felt as she sipped from Ettore's vein was a deeper blooming of desire.

It was the most erotic thing, to drink from him as he moved inside her, watching her with those eyes that burned everything away except the bond they now shared.

She didn't think her body could withstand another hot race toward climax, but Ettore's blood had unleashed something animal inside her. Something fierce and demanding. Something violently carnal.

"Ah, fuck, baby." He groaned, the tendons in his neck straining as she suckled his wrist and writhed beneath him. "I know. I can't be gentle now either."

Pulling his wrist away from her, he quickly sealed the wounds then flipped her over onto her stomach. One strong arm slid beneath her, hoisting her backside up to meet him as he slammed home from behind her.

He took her swiftly, aggressively, giving no quarter until they both were fully spent and collapsed on the bed in a sated tangle of limbs.

She didn't know how long they lay there, wrapped in each other's arms, their bodies slick with sweat and blood and the musky scent of their lovemaking. Bella could have stayed there for hours. Days. Forever.

She groaned when he rolled away, bringing her with him.

In the adjacent bathroom, the water began to run in the tub at

Ettore's mental command.

Bella rose off the bed with him, smiling as he caught her in his embrace and pressed a tender kiss to her forehead.

She drew back, searching the banked embers of his gaze. "That was...amazing."

He inclined his head in solemn agreement. "Yes, it was. More than amazing."

She traced one of the *dermaglyph* swirls on his chest. "So...where do we go from here?"

He grunted, a smile playing at the edges of his sensual mouth. "To the bathtub for starters. I've made a mess of you."

"No, Ettore." She slowly shook her head. "You've made me whole."

His expression intensified, sparking a soberness that she could feel now, in his blood. In her own blood too, as it throbbed heavily in her breast and in the pulse points that all craved his bite.

"Ah, Bella. God, I love you," he murmured. "But I don't know where we go from here. Back to Rome to begin with. From there, we'll have to figure it out. Right now, I only know that I need you with me."

It was all the promise she needed. Him. With her. Together.

She could hardly believe this was her new reality.

Tipping her chin up, he kissed her with reverent care. Then startled her when he scooped her into his strong arms and carried her to the bathroom. He stepped into the tub with her, sinking down into the water with her straddled against him.

Bella sighed into the comfort of his arms and the softly lapping pool around them. "This is heaven," she murmured, resting her head on the muscled pillow of his shoulder. "I've never been so happy. I never thought I would be."

Ettore tenderly caressed her, his hands wet and warm and soothing as he bathed her. She started to drift, her mind relaxing as she watched the little ripples dance in the bath water.

The vision came on so suddenly, she flinched.

It formed beneath the clear surface—horrific, bloody, violent.

She saw a Breed male covered in mangled, melted skin. Dark soot and grime smeared all over his shoulders and burned head. He held a screaming human in his jaws. The man's throat was torn open as the predator siphoned his blood in gulp after greedy gulp.

"Bella?" Ettore's voice was flat with dread.

He had to feel her shock. Her terror.

His hands shook as he pulled her away from him so he could see her face. Her gaze was still riveted on the water, her mind still caught in the hideous vision.

"Sweetheart, what is it? Tell me what's wrong."

She could hardly find the words.

Because at that moment, the Breed male in her mind's eye lifted his ruined head. His furious, blazing amber eyes seemed to reach out for her through the water.

"It's him," she murmured. "Massioni. He's alive."

Chapter 11

Bella's vision weighed on Savage like a ton of bricks parked on his chest, a weight that was only increasing in the hours since she'd described what she'd seen in the water. The very thing he'd dreaded, the mistake he'd made in not making sure he had finished the job, was soon coming home to roost. He had no doubt of that.

Unfortunately, Bella hadn't been certain if she'd seen Massioni in the immediate future, or days—even weeks—from now.

Nor did it matter.

The son of a bitch had survived the blast that should have killed him.

Vito Massioni was alive, and that meant Savage had failed in his mission for the Order.

He could only pray he hadn't failed Bella in the process.

And to make certain of that, he was doing the only thing he could think of to ensure their safety.

"Everyone ready to go, sweetheart?"

Bella nodded as she strode toward him from the back bedroom. "Chiara will be right behind me. She's having a bit of trouble with Pietro. The poor thing has been having nightmares most of the day."

"Understandable," Savage said. "The kid has been through quite an ordeal. You all have." He drew Bella under the shelter of his arm. "We need to be on the road to Rome as soon as the sun sets. It's only a few hours away, but the sooner I get you and your family there, the better I'll feel."

She peered up at him, stroking his tense jaw. "You're sure your comrades won't mind taking us in for a while?"

"You're my mate, Bella. Chiara and Pietro are my family now too. The command center may not be a suitable home for a child, but somehow we'll find a way to make it work."

Her gaze was tender on him. "You're a good man, Ettore."

"I want to be," he said. "For you. And that means making sure you're as far out of Massioni's reach as possible. At least until I can finish him for good."

Savage seethed with the urge to fix his fuck-up personally and painfully with the bastard. There was a time when he would have.

Before Bella reentered his life, he'd thought nothing of charging into the fray of a dangerous situation to take out a target. He'd never had a death wish, but as a warrior pledged in service to the Order, his life had been expendable if it meant the difference between success or failure of one of his missions.

All that had changed now. Bella and he were bonded. Now, if he were injured—if he were killed—she would feel his anguish as if it were her own.

She would suffer everything he did, just as he would endure her every pain or fear.

So, no matter how viciously he wanted to make Vito Massioni pay for every hour of every year he'd held Bella prisoner for his own gain, Savage had to exercise caution. He had to be sure he didn't fail—with her or with the Order.

She rested her head against his chest, where the heavy pound of his heartbeat throbbed. "I'm scared, Ettore."

"Don't be," he murmured, placing a kiss on the top of her head. "I'm not going to let him get you. I'm not going to let him get Chiara or her son either."

"I know you won't. But I'm scared for you." She drew in a shallow, ragged breath. "If I ever lose you again—"

"You won't." Guiding her gaze up to his, Savage urged her to see the resolve in his eyes. She had to feel it in her blood now, through the bond that would join them forever. He slid his hand around her nape and brought her to him for an unrushed kiss that ensured she felt all of the love and promise that he held for her in his heart.

He could have kissed her for hours, and he swore to himself that he would, once he made sure she and her family were safely returned to Rome.

Sensing they were no longer alone, Savage turned his head and found Scythe standing there. Christ, the male might be immense and formidable, but he moved like a wraith.

He held out his left hand, a vehicle starter in his palm.

"What's this?" Savage asked, pivoting to face the former Hunter. The key fob was for a Range Rover—a new one, by the look of it. Scythe handed it to him.

"The truck you arrived in might get you where you're going, but this will be better."

"I left that vehicle half a mile away at the church. How the hell did you know what we were driving?"

Scythe didn't answer, and Savage figured there was a lot about the reclusive male and his methods that would remain a mystery. Instead of pressing him, Savage slipped the welcome gift into his pocket.

"Thank you."

Scythe gave him a faint nod.

"We're ready!" Chiara called from behind them. "I'm sorry to keep you waiting."

The petite brunette had her son's little hand grasped in hers as she approached from the other end of the corridor. As they drew closer, Savage felt a cold shift in the air. He didn't realize what it was until he looked at Scythe and saw that the male had gone utterly still. His onyx eyes were stark, almost haunted, beneath the harsh slashes of his black brows.

Chiara must have felt the chill too. She glanced up nervously at Scythe, practically tugging dark-haired Pietro along when the boy's steps began to slow in front of the big Gen One.

But the child didn't seem to have any fear for the sinister-looking male. His feet halted in front of Scythe, his little head tilting up to stare in unabashed awe. "How'd you hurt your hand?"

Chiara and Bella both sucked in their breath. Hell, even Savage felt a jolt of unease as Scythe's hard gaze slowly descended to look at the boy. When he spoke, the male's deep voice was as unreadable as his stoic face.

"I tried to help someone a long time ago."

By the male's grave tone, Savage assumed his hand wasn't the only thing Scythe lost.

"Come on, Pietro." Chiara gave her son's hand a small tug. She looked up at the big male, her cheeks flaming with color. "I'm sorry. He's just starting to learn about manners."

Scythe shrugged vaguely, but his bleak eyes lingered on the pretty Breedmate. "It's all right."

Savage cleared his throat. "We should get moving. It's past sundown now, and we have a lot of time ahead of us on the road."

As he spoke, the faint sound of a woman's scream went up somewhere in the distance outside the *sassi*. Scythe heard it too. His dark head jerked to instant attention.

Just as another shriek sounded—this one closer and belonging to a man.

A man who was screaming for his life.

Savage's blood iced over with dread. "What the fuck?"

Scythe drew a phone out of his leather trench coat and brought something up on the display. His curse was guttural, vibrating with fury.

"Rogues," he said grimly.

He turned the device so Savage could see it. On the screen was live video from several different cameras positioned in Matera's city center. The surveillance showed humans racing in all directions, while a group of Rogues—he counted half a dozen in just the few seconds he watched—poured into the streets on the attack.

"Oh, my God," Bella gasped, her terror-filled eyes rooted to the small display.

It wasn't the first time in recent weeks that a city had been overrun by blood-addicted vampires. Thanks to Massioni's proliferation of Red Dragon, the narcotic that had turned scores of the Breed into Bloodlusting animals, violence like this was becoming almost epidemic again in many parts of the world.

Savage cursed viciously.

So much for leaving any time soon.

He wasn't about to risk Bella or anyone else's life by heading out into the chaos running rampant outside their safe house. And the idea of letting Matera's innocent population be slaughtered by blood-addicted predators was more than he could stand.

He met Scythe's fathomless black stare and saw the same resolve in him.

"You got extra weapons somewhere in here?"

The male gave him a curt nod.

More screams rang out in other parts of the town. More death coming closer by the minute. If the Rogues weren't stopped, it wouldn't take long before their attack moved down into the ravine.

Savage turned to Bella. He pulled one of his pistols from his weapons belt and placed it in her hand. "You ever shoot one of these?"

"No." She shook her head vigorously, but the worry he felt spiking through her blood was there for him. "Ettore, what are you—"

"Take it," he ground out fiercely, giving her a quick demonstration on how to take off the safety. "You aim this at anyone who comes to the door that isn't me or Scythe. And take this too." He unclipped a sheathed dagger from his belt and handed it to her. "That blade is titanium. It'll ash a Rogue in seconds flat."

He hoped to hell she never got close enough to one of them to use either of the weapons, but he wasn't taking any chances.

"Stay put, you hear me?" He grabbed her close, imploring her with his eyes and the hard, desperate pound of his heart. "I'll be back for you as soon as I can."

"Promise me."

He dragged her against him and kissed her—a brief, but impassioned confirmation that he wasn't about to lose her when they were so close to finally having a future together.

It wasn't easy to release her.

But as the terrorized screams of Matera's citizens continued to ring out, he knew he had little choice.

He turned to Scythe, now his unlikely ally. "Let's do this."

Chapter 12

The screams carrying down into the *sassi* from the city above only seemed to worsen in the few minutes after Ettore and Scythe had gone.

Those terror-filled shrieks—many of them agonized, final cries—left Bella shuddering and heartsick. Frightened to her marrow.

"We're going to be all right," she told Chiara and her frightened little boy, hoping her uncertainty didn't show in her eyes. As much as she trusted that Ettore was a capable warrior—Scythe too—they were only two against what was easily three times as many Rogues.

If anything happened to Ettore...

"You love him, don't you?" Chiara's voice was gentle, sympathetic.

"I love him more than anything in this world. I've loved him since I was a girl, back at the vineyard." She absently lifted her hand to the side of her neck, where she could still feel the claiming heat of Ettore's bite. "We're mated, Chiara. Our blood bond is only hours old."

"Oh, Bella." Chiara hugged her close. "You deserve this kind of happiness. You of all people deserve it."

Did she?

Bella couldn't help thinking that if not for her gift and Vito Massioni's want of it, Chiara and Pietro would not have been pawns at his mercy all these years. If not for her, Massioni would be dead—finished by Ettore in his mission for the Order.

If not for trying to rescue her from Massioni's villa, Ettore would already be back in Rome with his comrades, not swept into more violence and death.

High-pitched shrieks sounded again from somewhere outside.

"Momma!" Pietro whined, clutching at Chiara in wide-eyed alarm.

She picked him up and shushed him with tender words, rocking him. "It's okay, *piccolo*. Momma's here."

Bella reached out to stroke the little Breed male's head. "Why don't you both go relax in the back bedroom? It'll be quieter there."

Sheltered deeper into the cave dwelling. Away from the sounds of chaos and slaughter outside.

"You're sure?" Chiara gave her a dubious look. "I don't like the thought of leaving you alone to wait out here."

"Go," Bella gently encouraged. "I'll be fine. And soon Ettore and Scythe will be back."

Another sharp cry rent the night, startling Pietro. He started to cry softly against his mother's shoulder. Finally, on an apologetic nod, Chiara relented and turned to head back to the other room.

Bella took a seat in the living area, eyeing the weapons Ettore had given her. The gun and dagger rested on the side table next to her. She wished she were skilled enough to help him in some way. Feeling helpless made her antsy, made her mind spin from one disturbing thought to another.

She got up to pace the rug, worrying about Ettore. And the more she worried, the more she wondered if this random Rogue attack was actually random at all.

What if Vito Massioni had something to do with it?

She didn't want to think about the vision she had scried earlier, but the truth was his hideous face had been seared into her mind ever since.

And as much as she dreaded the idea of glimpsing him again, she needed to see if she could learn anything more that might help Ettore and the Order prepare to destroy him.

Taking the gun into the small kitchen with her, she retrieved a rustic stone bowl and filled it with water from the sputtering tap. Although Scythe didn't require mundane food or drink for nourishment as one of the Breed, his modest home had apparently been outfitted for human residents.

She stared into the bowl of water, trying to ignore all of the pain and death taking place outside her shelter. She focused all of her concentration on the clear pool, but nothing happened.

She tried again, praying for something.

Anything.

But the water gave her nothing.

Her gift refused to comply.

"Dammit." She heaved a sigh, closing her eyes and lowering her head into her palms.

When she opened them again, she did see a face reflected in the water.

Vito Massioni's hideous, disfigured face. His unblinking eyes stared back at her, the amber glow of them furious. Insane. Murderous.

His jaws were open, baring the twin daggers of his elongated fangs.

"Hello, Arabella."

Oh, God.

No.

She screamed and wheeled around, horrified to find the Breed male standing behind her. Her hand shot out to grab for the gun, but Massioni was much faster. With barely a sweep of his arm, he sent the weapon flying into the other room.

She tried to scramble out of his reach, but he grabbed a fist full of her long blonde hair and yanked her back. She crashed against him, her stomach turning at the foul stench of soured blood and death that clung to him.

"Didn't I warn you never to cross me, Bella?" His arms wrapped around her, strong as steel. His breath was hot and rank as it wormed into her ear. "Didn't I tell you there was nowhere you could run that I wouldn't find you? Your family too." He clucked his tongue, a revolting, wet sound. "Did you think I was so careless that I wouldn't take steps to make sure of that? The tracer on Chiara's truck led me straight to you. The Rogues ensured that the warrior from the Order would have no choice but to leave you unattended."

Nausea swamped her, not only from the horror of their mistake, but from the repulsiveness of Massioni's nearness. She moaned, struggling in vain to break loose. "Let me go!"

He chuckled. "Stupid girl. Didn't I tell you there would be pain if you deceived me? Now, there will be death."

Bella struggled and fought, but it was no use. Even severely injured from the blast that should have killed him, Massioni was inhumanly strong.

He was also deadly, even though his burned, mangled skin was raw, open wounds still seeping on his forearms despite the massive amount of blood he had likely consumed in his efforts to heal.

Bella's gaze fixed on the worst of the wounds that mangled the flesh of his arms. Maybe there was a tender spot on this dragon after all. Her bile churned, but she pushed past it to dig her fingers as deep and as savagely as she could into the ruined muscles and tendons.

He howled in anguish—and when his grasp loosened in reflex to the pain, she threw herself out of his grip. Stumbling to the floor, she scrambled away into the living area, hope surging through her.

But it was short-lived.

Chiara rushed out of the far chamber. "Bella? Oh, my God!"

Her scream when she spotted Massioni brought Pietro out of the bedroom behind her.

What happened next occurred so quickly, Bella could hardly comprehend it.

One moment, Massioni was doubled over in agony and anger. The next, he had Pietro by the wrist, holding the little boy up like a prize. Like a slab of meat caught on a butcher's hook.

Massioni's amber eyes burned even brighter in his rage. He snorted and sniffled, his lips peeling back from his teeth and fangs. There was a deep madness in his transformed gaze. In his feral, blood-stained face.

Oh, shit.

He really was crazy. Worse than crazy, but she hadn't realized it until now.

He had drunk too much blood since he escaped the blast.

Vito Massioni was lost to Bloodlust.

He was Rogue.

"You shouldn't have done that, Arabella. Now, you're really going to suffer."

His tongue slid out, snakelike, as he eyed the Breed child that dangled from his grasp. Then he looked back at her as she slowly got to her feet from her stumble into the other room.

His head cocked at a chilling, exaggerated angle. "I think we'll start by letting you watch me rip this boy's heart out and eat it in front of you both."

Chapter 13

"I don't think so, asshole."

Savage held a semiauto in his hand as he stood in the open doorway, his eyes lit up with fury, his fangs pulsing with the need to shred Vito Massioni to pieces.

He and Scythe had split up after leaving the *sassi*, working the attack from both ends of the city in order to contain the situation as best they could. Savage had just ashed his third Rogue of the night when all of a sudden it felt as if his heart was about to burst out of his chest in ice-cold terror.

Bella's terror.

Their bond had told him instantly that she was in danger. He hadn't been prepared for what he saw as he entered the *sassi* safe house and met with the hideous, Bloodlust-afflicted creature facing him now.

"Let the boy go, Massioni."

Savage would have opened fire already if Bella wasn't standing between him and a clear shot at the slavering Breed male.

Besides, in Massioni's current condition, he was as volatile as a human on PCP. Putting him down cleanly would take a lot more rounds than Savage had left in his pistol.

Or a titanium dagger.

Unfortunately, he'd buried one a few minutes ago in the skull of a Rogue who'd ripped the throat out of a nun inside one of Matera's old churches. His other blade he'd given to Bella.

He saw no trace of the gun or the knife he'd given her.

And there wasn't time to consider alternatives so long as Massioni had little Pietro hanging painfully by his wrist while Chiara wept and pleaded for mercy on her son.

Massioni sneered at Savage. "Done chasing rabbits so soon, warrior? Here I'd been looking forward to taking my time with these three."

"You heard me. Put the boy down."

Instead of complying, he raised Pietro higher, until the child's rib cage was level with Massioni's open maw. Saliva dripped from the tips of his fangs. "Put down your weapon, warrior."

Savage didn't move. He didn't as much as blink. Holding his 9mm steady, he only hoped Massioni would believe his bluff.

"Bella," he said calmly. "Move out of the way, baby."

Massioni growled. "Don't you take even one fucking step, Bella, or the next thing you'll hear is this brat's screams as I punch a hole through his sternum with my fist."

Chiara sobbed. Bella looked equally miserable, but she held herself together. She stared at Savage, shaking her head as if to warn him away from doing anything rash.

Well, fuck that. He would do anything to get her out of this, but damn if he wanted to forfeit an innocent child's life to accomplish it.

He saw little choice but to try to catch Massioni off guard.

In a split-second move, Savage took his shot, hitting the Breed male's forearm.

Massioni hissed as the bullet bit into his ravaged flesh.

As Savage hoped, he lost his grip on Pietro. The boy dropped to the floor, unharmed.

But then, just as quickly, Massioni snatched up Bella and hauled her against him like a shield.

She screamed. Arms trapped at her sides, she struggled in vain to break loose. The monster who held her only chuckled, seeming to delight in her terror. His glowing gaze was wild with madness. And dangerously smug triumph.

Savage couldn't contain the nasty curse that exploded out of him. He'd never known this kind of fear. He'd never felt the kind of bleak horror that raked him as he watched his mate sag into a resigned slump in her captor's arms.

Massioni tilted his head, those insane amber eyes studying Savage too closely.

"What's this?" he taunted. "Why, you look more than worried for this bitch, warrior. Am I taking something you thought belonged to you?"

"Let her go."

He held his weapon steady on his target, but he knew damned well he would never pull the trigger. Not when he was staring at Bella's beautiful, fear-stricken face.

If anything happened to her—for crissake, if she died right here at Massioni's hands—he would burn the whole world down around him.

"Please," he said woodenly, too afraid of losing her to care if he had to beg. "Let her go."

Massioni's eyes narrowed on him. "You've fucked her."

Savage bristled at the other male's crudeness. He wanted to flay him just for uttering the words.

A bark of laughter erupted from between the male's cracked and blistered lips. "Holy hell. You love her. Don't you, warrior?"

Bella made an anguished sound in the back of her throat. She shook her head at Savage, and as their eyes connected and held, he didn't so much feel fear in their bond, but a strange and steely determination.

"She's no good to me now," Massioni muttered. "Her gift was the only thing of value to me. You've ruined it." He shrugged. "I might as well kill her now."

Massioni gripped her chin in his soot-blackened, blood-stained fingers. He yanked her head back, and Bella's sharp cry tore into

Savage.

Her pain was real.

But her terror had galvanized into something else.

Something that told Savage to trust what he was feeling, not what he was seeing.

"All right." He relaxed his stance, lowering his weapon. "All right, you son of a bitch. You win."

Massioni stilled. Confusion swept over his feral features. His hold on Bella relaxed—ever so slightly.

It was all the opportunity she needed.

Twisting in the slackened cage of his arms, Bella drew the dagger she'd been concealing in her hand and drove it hard and fast and mercilessly into the center of his chest.

He staggered back, a look of shock on his face.

Until the poison of the titanium began to seep into his corrupted blood system. He howled, his face constricting in disbelief and agony. His body convulsed, collapsing to the floor.

Savage was at Bella's side in no time, pulling her close to him—holding her tight as the Rogue that had once been Vito Massioni began to disintegrate into a puddle of sizzling, melting flesh and bone.

In a few moments, there was only ash where his body had been.

He was dead, and Bella was safe.

Chiara and her son had come through the ordeal uninjured too.

As Savage held Bella in his embrace, he glanced to the door where Scythe had now entered. The former Hunter strode inside his house, his black gaze taking in the signs of struggle and the pile of ash still crackling on the floor. Then he looked to Chiara and Pietro, the pair of them huddled together nearby, and something crossed the remote male's face.

Relief, Savage thought.

And maybe something more.

Regret?

Whatever it was, the emotion was there and gone in an instant.

He gave Savage a sober nod, whether in confirmation of what he'd allowed him to see just then, or in acknowledgment of their teamwork tonight, Savage wasn't sure.

He might have tried to decipher it, but right then, with Bella warm and alive in his arms and his heart full to the brim with love for her, the only thing on his mind was the well-being of his woman.

His brave, beautiful mate.

He couldn't contain himself from dragging her to him for his kiss.

She resisted a little, drawing back on a small groan. "Ettore, I'm a mess. I have his blood on me…his foulness."

"That won't stop me from kissing you," he told her gently. "Nothing is going to stop me from doing that ever again."

He pulled her closer, wrapping her in his embrace as he brushed his lips over hers in a slower claiming, a tender joining of their mouths that still had the power to inflame them both—even after the ordeal they had just endured. Perhaps because of it too.

But she was right. She had been through hell with Massioni. Not only tonight, but for the past three years as well.

Now that the monster was no more, Savage wanted to erase all trace of him from Bella's life.

He swept his tongue across her soft lips on a groan that promised more. With Chiara quietly tending to her son, Savage lifted his head to look at Scythe.

"If you don't mind, I'd like to go draw a bath for my lady."

"Actually, I'd prefer a shower," Bella interjected, glancing up at him wryly. "No more baths, at least not for a while."

Savage chuckled. "Baby, whatever you want, it's yours."

"You, Ettore." Her soft brown gaze turned serious as she reached up and held his face in her warm, courageous hands. "You're all I want. You are all I'm ever going to need."

"You have me," he murmured quietly. "You have every part of me, sweet Bella. You always have."

They kissed again, his love for her soaring in his chest, in his veins. Through their bond.

Her love twined with his, and the depth of their connection was so profound it nearly brought him to his knees.

He didn't care that they had a small audience in the room with them. He didn't care who knew how completely he adored Arabella.

Loved her.

Desired her.

He wanted the whole world to understand that she was his.

And he was hers…in all ways.

Forever.

Chapter 14

"Keep kissing me like that, female, and I may decide to keep you here permanently."

Bella laughed and gazed up at Ettore, both of them now dried off and dressed after taking their time to clean up together. "Live in a *sassi* cave house and make little Breed babies? Sounds just about perfect to me."

Ettore paused. "Is that what you want?"

She smiled, lifted her shoulder in a faint shrug. "The cave is optional."

The sound he made as he wrapped his arms around her was one of joy and wonder. Even reverence.

"Do you have any idea how much I love you, Arabella?"

"I do," she said. "Because I feel it inside me. I hope you can feel even a fraction of the love I have for you, Ettore."

His rough moan was confirmation enough, but he kissed her anyway. Their union was so precious to her, she truly would have stayed right there with him forever if he asked it of her.

But Chiara and Pietro were waiting in the living area outside.

And Ettore's comrades with the Order in Rome were awaiting his return too.

Bella knew his duty was on his mind as he led her out to join the others. He'd been in touch with the command center in the hours since Massioni's death, both to inform them of the situation in Matera and to explain that he would be coming back to Rome with his Breedmate and her kin.

He threaded his fingers through hers as he brought her out to the main part of Scythe's home.

The signs of the earlier confrontation were gone now. Chiara was sweeping up the cold ashes from the floor, while Pietro sat on the rug nearby. He had a little toy in his hand—a carved lion made of stone. Scythe stood back from the boy, his black eyes haunted somehow as he watched him play with the miniature creature.

Bella's heart squeezed at the sight. When Scythe abruptly glanced up, she felt intrusive somehow. As if she had invaded private, long-buried thoughts that the forbidding Breed male had no intention of sharing.

Ettore held up the key that Scythe had given him earlier tonight. "Are you sure the Rover is ours?"

He gave a firm nod. "Keep it. If I have need of another vehicle, I have ample resources to get one."

"All right." Ettore inclined his head. "We should get moving, then. We have a lot of road ahead of us if we mean to make it back to Rome before sunrise."

Scythe grunted, contemplative. "Through my brother, Trygg, I'm aware that the Order has more than its share of trouble these days. If you or your comrades ever have need of more hands on deck—" The sober male actually smirked now. "Or even just one hand—then I trust you'll let me know."

Ettore chuckled. "I will. Thank you."

Scythe extended his good arm to him. The two males exchanged a brief left-handed shake. Then Scythe turned his fathomless gaze on Bella.

"Take care of each other."

"We will," she replied. And whether the intimidating Gen One wanted it or not, she rose up on her toes to kiss his beard-darkened face. "Thank you, Scythe. For everything you've done for us."

He stepped back without a word or acknowledgment, yet despite his reticence, she knew in her heart that she and Ettore had made a friend. If needed, they had a lethal, lifelong ally.

Chiara and her son as well.

Bella watched as her brother's widow collected her child from the rug where he was playing. She whispered something into Pietro's ear, then the boy shyly stepped over to stand in front of Scythe. In his pudgy fingers was the carved animal.

"Here," he said, offering it back to the larger male.

"You keep it," Scythe said, his deep voice toneless. "I've held on to it for too long. It's yours now."

Chiara smiled, gathering her arm around her little boy's shoulders. "I don't know how to thank you for giving us shelter," she murmured.

"No thanks is needed. It's enough to know that you and your child weren't harmed."

"No one's going to harm them anymore," Ettore added. "When I spoke with the command center, they informed me that the explosion at the villa the other night killed all of Massioni's lieutenants. His network is in shambles. My comrades and I are already making plans to crush his organization to the ground. No one will be coming after Bella or any of her family anymore."

Chiara's relief was clear in her eyes. But there was a note of hesitation there too. "I'm glad to hear that," she said. "Because I've decided that I don't want to go to Rome."

Bella frowned. "What? Then where—"

"The vineyard is my home, *sorella*. That's where Pietro and I belong."

Although it made sense, the thought of leaving her family behind still put a pang of sadness in her breast. Ettore must have registered the spike in her emotions. His fingers came to rest lightly under her chin, tipping her face up to meet his.

"Do you want the same thing, love? To go home to the vineyard, instead of living with me at the command center in Rome?"

"The vineyard hasn't been my home for a long time. Where you are, Ettore, that's my home now."

Because of him, her family was safe now.

Because of him, she had everything she'd ever wanted—all she needed—right here in her arms.

They said their final good-byes to Scythe, then drove his black Range Rover back to the vineyard in Potenza.

Hours later, with Chiara and Pietro settled again in their home, Ettore took Bella's hand and walked her out under the starlight.

She saw his gaze drift to the sleek blue Pagani that had brought them to this place two nights ago. It seemed like forever since he'd stormed into her life again and whisked her away from the villain who had held her.

Now, she and Ettore had forever waiting for them in their new life together.

She couldn't wait for it to begin.

He gestured to the sports car. "You don't suppose Chiara has any use for that, do you?"

"Hmm. Probably not," Bella replied with mock contemplation. "The Rover would be more practical. Not to mention it might give Scythe a reason to come around and check on them from time to time."

Ettore grunted. "I've got a feeling that might happen either way."

She smiled. "You may be right about that. Still, a sports car won't get much use out here at the vineyard. And Pietro is still years away from truly appreciating that kind of machinery."

"Shame to let a perfectly good Pagani sit unappreciated."

She smiled up at him. "And it'll certainly get us back to Rome a lot faster."

Ettore smirked. "Faster to Rome means faster into my arms again. And into my bed."

"I like the sound of that," she said, arching her brows.

"Then let's go."

He playfully smacked her backside, and they both raced down to the waiting car. They climbed in beneath the lifted gullwing doors, and in seconds the Pagani rumbled to life.

Ettore took her hand, bringing it up to his lips. "Ready for the ride of your life?"

"Oh, yes." Bella smiled. "I'm ready for anything with you."

* * * *

Also from 1001 Dark Nights and Lara Adrian, discover TEMPTED BY MIDNIGHT and STROKE OF MIDNIGHT.

Sign up for the 1001 Dark Nights Newsletter
and be entered to win a Tiffany Key necklace.

There's a contest every month!

Go to www.1001DarkNights.com to subscribe.

As a bonus, all subscribers will receive a free
1001 Dark Nights story
The First Night
by Lexi Blake & M.J. Rose

Turn the page for a full list of the
1001 Dark Nights fabulous novellas...

Discover 1001 Dark Nights Collection Three

HIDDEN INK by Carrie Ann Ryan
A Montgomery Ink Novella

BLOOD ON THE BAYOU by Heather Graham
A Cafferty & Quinn Novella

SEARCHING FOR MINE by Jennifer Probst
A Searching For Novella

DANCE OF DESIRE by Christopher Rice

ROUGH RHYTHM by Tessa Bailey
A Made In Jersey Novella

DEVOTED by Lexi Blake
A Masters and Mercenaries Novella

Z by Larissa Ione
A Demonica Underworld Novella

FALLING UNDER YOU by Laurelin Paige
A Fixed Trilogy Novella

EASY FOR KEEPS by Kristen Proby
A Boudreaux Novella

UNCHAINED by Elisabeth Naughton
An Eternal Guardians Novella

HARD TO SERVE by Laura Kaye
A Hard Ink Novella

DRAGON FEVER by Donna Grant

A Dark Kings Novella

KAYDEN/SIMON by Alexandra Ivy/Laura Wright
A Bayou Heat Novella

STRUNG UP by Lorelei James
A Blacktop Cowboys® Novella

MIDNIGHT UNTAMED by Lara Adrian
A Midnight Breed Novella

TRICKED by Rebecca Zanetti
A Dark Protectors Novella

DIRTY WICKED by Shayla Black
A Wicked Lovers Novella

A SEDUCTIVE INVITATION by Lauren Blakely
A Seductive Nights New York Novella

SWEET SURRENDER by Liliana Hart
A MacKenzie Family Novella

For more information, visit www.1001DarkNights.com.

Discover 1001 Dark Nights Collection One

FOREVER WICKED by Shayla Black
CRIMSON TWILIGHT by Heather Graham
CAPTURED IN SURRENDER by Liliana Hart
SILENT BITE: A SCANGUARDS WEDDING by Tina Folsom
DUNGEON GAMES by Lexi Blake
AZAGOTH by Larissa Ione
NEED YOU NOW by Lisa Renee Jones
SHOW ME, BABY by Cherise Sinclair
ROPED IN by Lorelei James
TEMPTED BY MIDNIGHT by Lara Adrian
THE FLAME by Christopher Rice
CARESS OF DARKNESS by Julie Kenner

Also from 1001 Dark Nights

TAME ME by J. Kenner

For more information, visit www.1001DarkNights.com.

Discover 1001 Dark Nights Collection Two

WICKED WOLF by Carrie Ann Ryan
WHEN IRISH EYES ARE HAUNTING by Heather Graham
EASY WITH YOU by Kristen Proby
MASTER OF FREEDOM by Cherise Sinclair
CARESS OF PLEASURE by Julie Kenner
ADORED by Lexi Blake
HADES by Larissa Ione
RAVAGED by Elisabeth Naughton
DREAM OF YOU by Jennifer L. Armentrout
STRIPPED DOWN by Lorelei James
RAGE/KILLIAN by Alexandra Ivy/Laura Wright
DRAGON KING by Donna Grant
PURE WICKED by Shayla Black
HARD AS STEEL by Laura Kaye
STROKE OF MIDNIGHT by Lara Adrian
ALL HALLOWS EVE by Heather Graham
KISS THE FLAME by Christopher Rice
DARING HER LOVE by Melissa Foster
TEASED by Rebecca Zanetti
THE PROMISE OF SURRENDER by Liliana Hart

Also from 1001 Dark Nights

THE SURRENDER GATE By Christopher Rice
SERVICING THE TARGET By Cherise Sinclair

For more information, visit www.1001DarkNights.com.

About Lara Adrian

LARA ADRIAN is the *New York Times* and #1 internationally best-selling author of the Midnight Breed vampire romance series, with nearly 4 million books in print and digital worldwide and translations licensed to more than 20 countries. Her books regularly appear in the top spots of all the major bestseller lists including the *New York Times*, *USA Today*, *Publishers Weekly*, Indiebound, Amazon.com, Barnes & Noble, etc.

Lara Adrian's debut title, Kiss of Midnight, was named Borders Books best-selling debut romance of 2007. Later that year, her third title, Midnight Awakening, was named one of Amazon.com's Top Ten Romances of the Year. Reviewers have called Lara's books "addictively readable" (Chicago Tribune), "extraordinary" (Fresh Fiction), and "one of the best vampire series on the market" (Romantic Times).

With an ancestry stretching back to the Mayflower and the court of King Henry VIII, Lara Adrian lives with her husband in New England, surrounded by centuries-old graveyards, hip urban comforts, and the endless inspiration of the broody Atlantic Ocean.

Connect with Lara online:

Website - http://www.laraadrian.com/
Facebook - https://www.facebook.com/LaraAdrianBooks
Twitter - https://twitter.com/lara_adrian
Pinterest - http://www.pinterest.com/laraadrian/

Discover More Lara Adrian

Stroke of Midnight
A Midnight Breed Novella
By Lara Adrian

Born to a noble Breed lineage steeped in exotic ritual and familial duty, vampire warrior Jehan walked away from the luxurious trappings of his upbringing in Morocco to join the Order's command center in Rome.

But when a generations-old obligation calls Jehan home, the reluctant desert prince finds himself thrust into an unwanted handfasting with Seraphina, an unwilling beauty who's as determined as he is to resist the antiquated pact between their families.

Yet as intent as they are to prove their incompatibility, neither can deny the attraction that ignites between them. And as Jehan and Seraphina fight to resist the calling of their blood, a deadly enemy seeks to end their uneasy truce before it even begins....

Tempted By Midnight
A Midnight Breed Novella
By Lara Adrian

Once, they lived in secret alongside mankind. Now, emerged from the shadows, the Breed faces enemies on both sides—human and vampire alike. No one knows that better than Lazaro Archer, one of the eldest, most powerful of his kind. His beloved Breedmate and family massacred by a madman twenty years ago, Lazaro refuses to open his heart again.

Sworn to his duty as the leader of the Order's command center in Italy, the last thing the hardened warrior wants is to be tasked with the rescue and safekeeping of an innocent woman in need of his protection. But when a covert mission takes a deadly wrong turn, Lazaro finds himself in the unlikely role of hero with a familiar, intriguing beauty he should not desire, but cannot resist.

Melena Walsh has never forgotten the dashing Breed male who saved her life as a child. But the chivalrous hero of her past is in hard contrast to the embittered, dangerous man on whom her safety now depends. And with an unwanted—yet undeniable—desire igniting between them, Melena fears that Lazaro's protection may come at the price of her heart....

Defy the Dawn

Don't miss the newest novel in the *New York Times* bestselling Midnight Breed series by Lara Adrian!

On sale now in eBook, print, and audiobook.

Enjoy this sneak peek!

"What do you want, Zael?" Brynne frowned, folding her arms militantly across her chest. "And just what the fuck do you think you're doing, barging into my private quarters like this?"

At the moment, the only thing he was doing was staring at her, slack-jawed and instantly aroused. She stood in front of him half-dressed in just her white button-down shirt she'd worn that night in London. Her long legs were bare, exposing the delicate swirls and flourishes of her Breed *dermaglyphs* that tracked down her slender thighs. The silky stems with those pretty, feminine *glyphs* seemed to go on forever.

Beneath the loose hem of her blouse, he caught a tantalizing glimpse of skimpy black panties and more creamy skin. God, she was beautiful. Exotic and strong and exquisitely female.

She was also visibly pissed off. At him?

"What's going on here, Brynne?"

She stood her ground, glowering at him. "Isn't it obvious? I'm getting dressed."

From where he was standing, it looked like she was getting undressed. And there were certain parts of his anatomy that approved of that idea very enthusiastically.

"You said you're leaving."

"Yes. I have to go back to London. That's where I belong." She turned away and began buttoning her shirt the rest of the way as she stalked to the bed. The pair of dark navy slacks she'd been wearing the other night lay folded there. Her shoes and purse were gathered nearby as well. "I mean to be on that plane with Mathias Rowan and the others later today."

Zael frowned at the announcement. "Don't you think we should talk?"

"About what?"

Was she serious? He didn't even know where to begin. "About this new Opus attack. About where you and I fit into the equation with the Order. We sure as hell need to talk about what's happening between us."

"Nothing's happening between us, Zael." Sharp words, delivered with a flare of amber in her dark green eyes as she threw a hard glance at him from over her shoulder. "As for the rest of it, you heard Lucan and the other warriors just now. You saw what's going on all around us. The whole world is going to hell right now."

"Yes," he agreed. "And it's going there regardless of what takes place between you and me."

She scoffed. "You'll say anything to get what you want, won't you? Is that how all the men of your kind operate? I suppose that explains all of the fatherless offspring you and the rest of your Atlantean brothers have left around the world."

Zael's jaw hardened at the jab. It wasn't completely without merit, but he also saw it for what it was. A defensive strike, meant to push him away.

She pivoted away from him again, as if she was finished with their conversation and finished with him. Maybe that ice-cold shoulder had been enough to shut out all of the other men who tried to get close to Brynne, but not him.

He'd seen the desire in her eyes when they had nearly kissed today. He'd felt her soften in his arms in that moment, not only resigned to the need that they both felt, but consumed by it with the same intensity that it owned him.

She flinched when he came up behind her and put his hands on her shoulders. She stiffened under his touch, but he could feel the heavy spike of her pulse, and the sudden, rapid rhythm of her breathing. "If you're so hell-bent on running away, at least be honest about it. You're running away from me."

"I'm sure you'd like to think so."

"No, Brynne. I don't want you to run away from me." He swore, low under his breath, and he turned her around to face him. Her mouth was set in a firm line, but her glittering eyes softened as he held her. "I should be glad that you want to run away from me, from this. I should want that as badly as you seem determined to go."

To his astonishment, she trembled as the seconds stretched out between them. Bold, defiant, hard-headed Brynne stared at him in silent trepidation. She licked her lips, and he glimpsed the sharp white points of her fangs.

"I told you earlier that I didn't want anything to do with you, Zael." Desperation crept into her voice. "Why can't you accept that? Why can't you just leave me alone?"

"Because every time I look at you, I see the same desire in your eyes that I feel burning me up inside."

He brought one hand up to stroke the softness of her cheek. Pinkness rose into her face as his thumb flicked across her parted lips. It made her look so fragile, almost innocent. The color spread downward, along the delicate column of her throat, then into the open collar of her shirt and across the pretty swells of her breasts.

Yes, Brynne Kirkland was hard-shelled and stubborn. Yes, she was a lethally powerful creature, born of a race his own had long feared and despised. But beneath her *dermaglyph*-covered skin, she was a woman. A woman who yearned for a man's touch.

His touch.

"Wanting you this way is the last thing I should be doing, Brynne. But I'm not going to stand here and lie to you by pretending there's nothing between us." He caught her face in his palms. "I'm not going to stand here and let you lie about that either."

"Zael—" She moaned the instant their mouths met. Her hands flattened against his shoulders, but it wasn't to push him away. As he took her deeper into his kiss, Brynne's fingers curled into the loose white linen of his shirt. She clung to him, her body telling him everything her words could not.

He growled low and possessive into her mouth as he pushed his tongue inside to meet hers. Her breath raced hot and heavy. The tips of her fangs grazed his lips as he claimed her hungrily, demanding her surrender. And she gave it to him.

Holy fuck, did she ever.

That kiss they'd been denied a short while ago only made the heat reignite all the hotter now.

Their mouths joined in undeniable need, Zael skimmed his hands over her arms, then traced his fingers along her sides. She shivered as he slid his palms under her blouse and onto the soft, bare skin of her torso.

The intricate lines of her *glyphs* throbbed beneath his fingertips, warm and pulsing. Unearthly and alive. Their pattern created a tempting, tactile roadmap across her belly and rib cage—one he craved to follow with his tongue.

He wanted to uncover and devour every sweet inch of her body.

But first, he wanted to hear her say the words.

"Now tell me there's nothing happening between us," he rasped against her kiss-swollen lips.

As he spoke, Zael reached around her and deftly unfastened her bra. The lacy cups slackened, freeing her naked breasts into his hands. She sighed deeply as he caressed her. Moaned sharply as he rolled the tight beads of her nipples between his fingers.

"Tell me you haven't been wanting this as much as I have, Brynne."

Her pleasured gasp tore out of her without resistance, but it wasn't good enough.

Pushing her shirt and bra out of the way, he bent his head and pulled one rosy nipple into his mouth. Each tug of his tongue and lips made the colors of her *dermaglyphs* intensify, their patterns churning and transforming in response to her rising desire. Brynne arched against him as he sucked and licked her. Her spine bowed, she plunged her fingers into his hair, her legs trembling beneath her.

The scent of her arousal filled his nostrils. Spicy and sweet. Ethereal and bold. Like earth and heaven combined.

Damn, she was lovely. Sexy as hell. Although he had bedded many women over his long lifetime, he had never been with a woman who was Breed. He never imagined he could want any woman the way he wanted Brynne.

The cynical part of him tried to dismiss this need he felt for Brynne as nothing more than sexual novelty, just his libido craving a new diversion. But if that had been the case, he never would have denied her back in London. Refusing her had been one of the hardest things he'd ever done. And he wasn't about to let her act as if he was alone in that torment.

"Tell me you want me, Brynne. Tell me what you said to me the other night on that dance floor. Now, when there's no whisky to hide behind. Nothing but you and me, and the truth between us."

He skated one hand down the length of her body, into the parted cleft of her thighs. The tiny scrap of black silk that covered her sex was soaked and so hot against Zael's fingertips he groaned with the need to touch her, to taste her…to brand himself on all of her senses.

He cupped his hand over her mound, one finger slipping beneath her panties to the silken heat of her naked folds. Her sex was slick and lush, her juices coating his fingertips as he caressed her swollen folds and the hardened bud of her clit.

"Tell me now," he said, "when you can't take it back later or tell me I'm insane for thinking you feel this need too."

She whimpered, a tremor shuddering through her as he stroked her wet satin flesh. He teased the tight entrance of her sex, stopping just shy of penetration, despite that her thighs clamped tight around his hand in unspoken demand.

He wanted to hear her admit the truth out loud, once and for all.

"Say it, Brynne. Tell me you haven't been wanting to feel me inside you from the moment we first saw each other right outside on that terrace last week."

She made an anguished sound and he glanced up to find her eyes blazing with fiery amber, her Breed pupils narrowed to thin slits. Her fangs gleamed from behind the plush line of her upper lip.

She was beautiful under normal circumstances, but like this, she was primal and otherworldly, so fiercely sexy that she defied any description.

Holding his gaze, Brynne licked her lips and the truth boiled out of her in a single word. *"Yes."*

On behalf of 1001 Dark Nights,

Liz Berry and M.J. Rose would like to thank ~

Steve Berry
Doug Scofield
Kim Guidroz
Jillian Stein
InkSlinger PR
Dan Slater
Asha Hossain
Chris Graham
Pamela Jamison
Fedora Chen
Jessica Johns
Dylan Stockton
Richard Blake
BookTrib After Dark
The Dinner Party Show
and Simon Lipskar

CPSIA information can be obtained
at www.ICGtesting.com
Printed in the USA
LVOW11s2254040517
533267LV00003B/572/P

9 781942 299592